I0457184

Fairy Tales
Refocused

Different takes on familiar tales

LYNDA DUNWELL

Publisher's note:
This book is a work of fiction. Names, characters, places and incidents either are the product of the author's imagination or are used fictitiously, and any resemblance to actual persons, living or dead, business establishments, events or locales is entirely coincidental.

The publisher does not have any control over and does not assume any responsibility for author or third-party websites or their content.

Thanks to the dedicated team at Romantic Reads Publishing, editors Betty Turner and Maggie Glynn, also fellow author and beta reader Heidi McAnna.

Cover Design: Selfpubbookcovers.com/Ravenborn

CONTENTS

WANTED NEW MAN

Clad in his motorbike leathers Fred stomped into the kitchen. "I'll just change," he said.

"If only you would," mouthed Gemma under her breath as she heard him climb the stairs. She returned to her shopping list, sorely tempted to add *new man* beneath the groceries. List done, she went to the foot of stairs and shouted, "Nearly ready Fred?"

No reply.

She shouted again, waited a few moments then went after him. She entered the bedroom, halted and let out a loud gasp. "Fred! There's a big frog on our bed. Come and get rid of it now!"

No reply.

"Fred, where are you? If this is one of your practical jokes, it isn't funny!"

The frog croaked.

Gemma stepped around the creature and yanked open the wardrobe. Fred's clothes hung there, but no Fred. "Are you hiding? Am I supposed to find you?" She made a big show of looking in all the usual places until fed up, she collapsed onto the bed. "Okay, I give in, where are you?"

Throughout Gemma's performance the frog hadn't moved except for puffing out his throat and eyeballing her.

"What happens now?" She glared at him. "Croak once for yes and twice for no?"

It was meant to be a snide remark but, obligingly, the frog croaked once.

"Am I supposed to believe you're Fred?"

"Croak."

"Do I look stupid? Men don't suddenly turn into frogs. You're watching me, aren't you? And laughing at me talking to a frog. Fred, come out at once!"

"Croak, croak."

Gemma stormed downstairs. The shopping list lay on the kitchen table where she had left it. She rushed to the window and expected to see an empty drive. Fred had gone out, she tried to convince herself and somehow she had missed him. But the car was there next to Fred's bright green motorbike.

She folded her arms and stomped back to the foot of the stairs. "You won't catch me out," she shouted. "I'm not bothered. I'm going to play on-line bingo."

She didn't have time to log onto her

favourite site as the frog hopped onto the keyboard. "Ugh!" she screamed and ran into the kitchen.

Later, when her nerves had settled, she crept back to the computer. The frog was still sitting there in front of a message on screen supposedly from Fred. *Jumped onto bed and have been turned into frog.*

"Really?" Gemma sniggered. "And a wicked witch has cast a spell on you, what a shame."

The frog pressed a few keys and *dunno* appeared on the screen.

"Look, frogs in fairy tales can talk, why can't you?"

Can't...help me flashed up.

"How?" she shrugged.

The story, what happens?

"Simple, the princess kisses him and, bingo, he's back as the prince."

Kiss me then!

"I don't think so!"

Please...

Reluctantly Gemma touched the frog's slimy face with her finger and lowered her lips to meet his. "Yuk!" she cried jumping back.

Nothing happened.

Try again, please?

"This is gonna cost you Fred. This isn't a joke anymore, I've had enough."

Please, Gemma, please...I'll love you

forever...promise.

Pressing her lips together, Gemma kissed the frog again. No result. Standing back, she said, "Perhaps I've got the story wrong? I'll google it."

Within seconds a version of the fairy tale was on screen. "Okay, the princess owes the frog a favour, so she offers him a home with her, never thinking he'd bother to move in. When he shows up, she gets angry, grabs him and throws him against a wall. He turns back into a prince and they live happily ever after."

Is that it?

"Yes."

Sounds painful. Can you try?

"No way! This really has gone far enough...and you're probably filming everything or worse...putting it all on the net. I can't harm a defenceless creature. It's wrong. This is another of your sad jokes Fred, isn't it? Frog, I don't know how you got in my house but you are so out of here!" Using both hands she scooped up the frog, carried him into the garden and deposited him on the lawn.

That night Gemma slept alone. Fred didn't show up. By next morning she was worried and talking to herself. "What can I do? People will think I'm crazy if I tell them my partner has turned into a frog and wants to be thrown against a wall."

The next couple of days she cleaned the house from roof space to ground level, mowed the lawn and weeded the flower borders. On the third night she went to a neighbour's barbeque.

"Fred's away," she said when people asked.

"On, never mind, come and meet my French cousin, Henri," said the hostess, "he's a chef."

"This chicken's delicious," said Gemma and picked up another bite-size piece from the platter Henri handed around.

"Not chicken," he insisted, "but the finest frogs' legs I've cooked in years. You English, why don't you eat them?"

"Maybe we don't know how to cook them," Gemma shrugged.

"Poaching is best. These frogs are from the garden. They're good because they're so fresh."

They were the first frogs' legs Gemma ate, but not the last. When she reported Fred missing at the police station, she didn't mention the frog incident. Occasionally, she wonders what really happened to him as she's not heard from him since. But she's not bothered because now she is living happily with Henri.

PUSS AND THE POLE DANCER

Her four inch high heels flashed silver like daggers piercing the ground but she smelt nice, so I followed her. She stopped at the back entrance to Smilies Club, a seedy dark place by the riverbank on the wrong side of town. I knew it well, Fred the doorman regularly gave me scraps, so I hung around after she went inside.

I glanced around, too early for the river rats and the dogs had gone hunting further down river by the market place, it being Friday.

The door opened and I slipped inside. I'd been in the club before, not that it was the sort of place I normally frequented, too many sweaty fat middle-aged men who certainly weren't cat lovers. I sat down on my haunches, glanced around and kept my ears pricked. Along the dark corridor another door opened, just enough for a slender feline like me to gain access. I blinked several times, getting my eyes accustomed to the brightness and the colours.

Racks of feathery, sparkly garments hung on plastic hangers. Four large mirrors lined with electric light bulbs covered one wall above a long table where pots of make-up stood stacked up side by side. I crept under the table and hid in the corner away from the legs of the only occupant, the woman with the silver heels.

A near naked young woman charged in, slammed the door behind her and flopped down on one of the chairs. All she wore were her spiky red platform heels and a matching shiny thong.

"There's a bloody riotous crowd in tonight, Friday night stags. Think they're up for anything! Bleeding cheek, watch the red haired yobbo in the front at the end pole, Thinks he's some sort of porno star, flashing his cock at me, made a grab for my tits when I was hanging upside down. Watch him. I'd have poked his eyes out with my spikes given half a chance."

"And got the sack at the same time," silver heels said.

"Perhaps, but I've had it up to here with

this place. I've saved enough for the plane, I'm off to Spain at the end of the month."

"When will you tell Jason?"

"I'm not going to and don't you go spilling the beans. As soon as he's paid me, I'm out of here."

Silver heels didn't say anymore, I guess she was due to do her act or whatever they called it when they wrapped themselves around poles. I watched her get up and slowly sashay towards the door. That's when I slipped out, I wanted to hide in the club and watch her. There was something about her that appealed to my feline intuition.

The music started soft and low as she began twisting slowly around the pole. Using first one hand and then the other to propel herself around, she started to slowly remove what little clothing she was wearing. Each time a piece of silver fabric was stripped off, the audience cheered and the music changed pace. Like her companion earlier she eventually got down to a triangle of silver fabric around her crotch and those spiky shoes. She wriggled and swung around the metal pole so many times, I was surprised she didn't get giddy and fall off. But she stayed there, sometimes doing incredible things like the splits and bending her head onto her knees. Yeah, she sure was a very supple girl.

I continued to watch her twirl, pose and

wrap her lithe body around the shiny pole. Men, sometimes two or three deep, ogled her but she seemed oblivious to their noise and remained straight-faced. Not a glimmer, smirk or even a slight pretence at a smile showed on her face. Hence I got the impression she didn't like her job. Perfect for me.

It was a pity some of her audience didn't appreciate her gymnastic ability but they seemed content to make rude gestures, laugh at their own jokes and generally try to score points off their mates by jeering and boasting about their own male prowess and what they would like to do to her.

She finished her performance as the music faded, slipped off her pole, did a bow for the audience and left the podium. I followed and kept as close to her spiky heels as I dared. She opened the door of the dressing room. It was empty, red heels must have left. I slipped inside and sat down as she collapsed onto a chair.

"How would you like to get out of this place?" I said.

"Who's there?" she asked in a startled voice.

"Me – Puss, down here."

"What the ....?"

"Yes I know it's a bit of a shock to hear a talking cat, but I am one. Although only people I want to hear me can. You're special. What's your name?"

"Desire..."

"Nice name but that's what that guy announced you as, now what's your real name?"

"Julie."

"OK Julie, here's the deal." I jumped up onto her dressing table and squatted on my haunches. "I am a special cat. I have a few special powers, not magic, but my feline intuition is finely tuned. I need a female human to work with me. I've tried working with men. My last protégé worked hard as first but when he grew richer he forgot who had been responsible for his early success. In short, he thought he could do without me, neglected me and left me behind when he went on a business trip."

"Yeah, I know the feeling. I've been with guys like him. That's how I ended up here when I got thrown over and chucked out." But this isn't some sort of set up, is it? Hell, don't tell me I'm live on the net."

"No Julie you're not – watch my mouth. Ever seen a cat talk like me? Do you think for one second I want my talking skills broadcast to the world? I'd be locked up, x-rayed and maybe dissected until all those so-called clever scientists had had their fill. No Julie, I'm talking to you because you are special and I think we can do business together."

She thought for a few moments, then said, "Right Puss, what am I to do?"

Great, it looks like Julie and I are making progress. "First we're getting out of this place now. Do you have any money?"

"A few quid, my wages for tonight, but it won't go far."

"Never mind, get dressed we're going to Max's Casino. He never runs straight tables but I can get you on a winning streak, if you can hide me in your handbag."

"That won't do Puss, they'll search me when I go in."

"Yes, so I'll go around the back and squeeze through an open door or window. If I go into the games room the CCTV will spot me, so pick me up in the ladies. I'll hide in your bag and then follow my instructions for the roulette wheel."

Bless her shiny spikes and the silver thong she was still wearing as we came out of Max's a couple of thousand up. Julie was well-pleased and took me back to her flat, actually it was a bedsit.

"What have I done to deserve you?" she asked as she counted the winnings.

"Nothing, let's say last night was your lucky day."

"Would you like to drink, milk?"

"Hell no! Where do humans get the idea

that felines love milk? Gives me bellyache. Some chicken would be nice, or raw mince or fish, oh, I also eat mice, preferably live."

"OMG! You eat mice!"

"Of course, I'm a cat, aren't I?"

She found some cold chicken in her fridge and gave it to me. When I'd finished she ran her finger along the side of my jaw. It sent powerful sensations down my spine. "Meow, that's so nice."

"So what's next?" she asked.

"A few hours sleep," I said yawning. So I settled down on her bed pleased we had had a successful evening. Our future together looked good.

We didn't go back to Max's or the pole dancing club but we did boost our funds at a few more casinos before hitting the bright lights in London. Julie scrubbed up rather well. With her new clothes, hairstyle and a few pieces of jewellery, all chosen by yours truly, she could get into some of the best clubs. She had a special carrier made for me and I got a diamante collar.

Her reputation as a professional gambler grew. She was recognised by all the doormen and attracted attention from the club owners.

"You're becoming too well known," I said to her over breakfast.

"Yes, I've noticed. The tables aren't going so well for us. It's as if they see me coming. One manager, Gino Patrico suggested I shouldn't play at his table again. He accused me of having a formula. Yeah, I said, like Puss tells me the numbers to play."

"Hmm...time to fry fresher fish I think. What about politics?"

Julie nearly choked on the piece of toast she was eating. "What? I've not got a clue, wouldn't know which party to support. I've never voted in my life."

"Good," I said, "you could stand as an independent, not Parliament, not at first but the local council. You don't get paid only expenses but our funds are quite large, I think it's time to do some good. How about taking up women's rights? Campaign for street girls, fight exploitation and human trafficking."

"That means doing speeches I'm not up to that. Besides, once I step into the media's spotlights I'll get slated for my pole-dancing."

"Great, what a platform. Don't you see? You could campaign for the underdog. I can help with the speeches as long as I'm by your side."

Julie ran her finger along my jaw line and rubbed that special place below my ear. "Puss, I want you to always be at my side because I love you."

Well, that made me feel quite

embarrassed, but cats can't blush. OK, I'd been shown affection before but never did anyone actually say they loved me. The feeling felt good.

Julie stood for the local council election and we worked together on raising issues like homelessness, vagrancy and championing the lot of the less fortunate. She was popular, very persuasive and became a formidable force to be reckoned with in London.

One day, after Julie had been on the council for over two years, I suggested to her it was time to move on.

"Oh, no Puss, you're not leaving me!" she cried almost near to tears. "I love you, there is no one in the world more important to me than you."

I rubbed my head against her arm. "No, silly," I said, "only it's time we moved onward and upward in the world."

"What do you mean?"

"I'm not getting any younger, I'm twelve years old, that's eighty-four in your lifespan. I won't live forever."

"Oh, no, whatever will I do without you?"

"Fear not, you're wise, you have a good heart and you care about people. Those qualities won't leave you when I'm no longer around. Don't you want a family of your own?"

"Not whilst I have you Puss, you are my family."

Of course I was flattered although it had never been my plan to have so much affection showered upon me. From the beginning I wanted to help Julie because to me she was special.

"You have a lot of love to give," I told her. "I'm sure you can find a man who is worthy of you."

"Perhaps but there's no time, there's so many poor people who need help."

"What if you were asked to be Chairman of the Council perhaps you could do more for the poor people?" I watched Julie's face usually I could read her thoughts before she said a word. I could see she was confused.

"I don't think I could."

"Nonsense, you can do anything."

"Only with your help," she sighed.

A week later several of her fellow councillors suggested she stood for the chair. At first she was flattered but refused. I talked her into accepting by promising to help her.

One year later, Julie was approached to stand as an independent candidate for Mayor of London.

"How can I stand?" she asked me.

"Very easily, you will be the youngest

Mayor of London in history and with your track record helping so many unfortunates in the capital, I'd be surprised if you didn't win by a large majority.

Julie did win and me? I stayed with her, proud of my protégé. You can come a long way in life with the help of a talking cat – if you are lucky enough to find one.

NEW SHOES

"Mirror, mirror on the wall, where are the most beautiful shoes of all?"

Pure self-indulgence but we had to ask the question, although we knew the answer because we were the only pair of crystal high-heels in the kingdom. Of course the mirror didn't reply. Mirrors are silent, they simply reflect but in our case the reflection is spectacular.

We are displayed in the window of Posh and Polish, the most prestigious shoe shop in the land. And as our establishment only caters for the most important people in the realm, we have been granted a Royal Charter. That means we make and fit the queen and most of the royal court with the most expensive and finest footwear in the world. And we are the most beautiful shoes ever made.

One day an old woman hobbled into Posh and Polish. Clarice, our senior shop assistant, immediately twitched her nose because it was obvious that someone of the old woman's social standing couldn't possibly afford even the cheapest slippers in our shop.

"Can I help you?" Clarice asked.

The old woman stared at her. "No dear, I don't think there is anything you can do for me or me for you." She turned away and fixed her eyes upon us. A cold shiver ran the length of our left and right spines. It was so severe it clicked noisily as it emerged from our exquisite heels.

"Oh no!" right shoe cried. "She can't possibly have come in here to buy us!"

"Don't be silly," left shoe sneered. "She can't afford us."

"I'd like those crystal slippers," the old woman said.

We froze and nearly turned to ice despite Clarice's warm hands around us. She lifted us out of the window, first left, then right. "Are you sure," she asked, "only these are our finest and therefore our most expensive shoes."

"Yes, we're expensive, tell her that," we squeaked. "Then she'll say she can't afford us and leave and we won't have to go with her to goodness knows where, and we can stay here where everyone admires us."

"How much?" the old woman asked.

"Ten thousand guilders," Clarice replied.

"Cheap at twice the price!" The old woman's mouth widened exposing her black teeth. She took out a pouch from under her cloak and tipped the contents onto the shop counter. With her bony fingers she counted out the money. "Ten thousand in gold."

Before we knew what was happening we were boxed up and tucked under the old woman's black cloak. We had no idea where she took us, although we did our best to keep each other in good spirits as we lay in the dark in our box.

Sometime later we heard her talking about some ball and promising someone that they would be going.

"But I can't go like this," a young girl's voice said.

"Of course not, my dear," the old woman replied as a sound like the wind whistling through trees came for apparently nowhere.

"But how can I get to the palace?" the young girl asked. "The ball must have started as my stepmother and sisters left ages ago."

"Fear not," the old woman said, "I have the perfect transportation waiting outside. Look through the window."

"A crystal coach," the young girl

exclaimed. "What have I done to deserve these wonderful gifts?" she asked.

"You have a good heart," the old woman replied, "and you are always kind to others, no matter what their station in life might be. You have a lot of love in your heart and I have come to make your dreams come true."

"Can't she make our dreams come true and get us out of this dam box," left shoe said.

"Try to be patient," right shoe urged. "I'm sure some good is going to come out of this."

"Yeah, sure, think that if it makes you feel good," left added.

"Shush," right whispered, "they're talking again."

"But before you go," the old woman said, "there's one more thing..."

"Listen left shoe, pray with me, please, please patron saint of shoes, whoever you are, let her mean us...let her get us out of here!"

Whosh! The lid of our box flew off.

"Wow!" right shoe cried. "We must remember to pray to that saint again. At last we can breathe. Okay, look smart, twinkle if you can."

"I'm doing my best," left moaned.

"These slippers are for you my dear, they are special," the old woman said. "Wear them and your dreams will come true. But remember, my powers only last until midnight, you must leave the ball by the last stroke of twelve or my gifts will return to their former selves."

"Former selves? What does she mean?" left asked. "We're not former selves. We're the most beautiful pair of glass slippers in the world, aren't we?"

Right shoe nodded.

We were on her feet and nice lovely slender small feet they were too, and it was a real pleasure to ride in a crystal coach. We had no idea she was so grand and royal. At last we had been raised to our proper place and were on our way to a grand ball.

It didn't take us long to reach the palace where a right royal shin-dig was underway. Crowds of people, all dressed up in their finery, were being presented to the King and Queen, who were supported by their only son, the Prince.

We could only see him from the ground upwards but what we saw was most pleasing. He wore a very smart pair of white leather boots – Posh and Polish of course. We remembered when they were made and greeted the boots most affably. We danced every dance with them and when they led us out onto the terrace and stepped close, we welcomed the feeling of their soft leather against our hard crystal.

Then we heard it. That bloody great clock in the palace courtyard had begun to dong twelve. What was happening? We were in flight, running as fast as we possibly could.

"Heavens! Give us a break, young lady, we're made of crystal glass," we screeched in unison.

The young woman must have thought she was wearing a pair of running shoes not the most beautiful crystal shoes of all. Couldn't she tell that each step she took over the hard ground reverberated painfully along our spines?

"I can't stand this anymore," left shoe cried.

"Hang on, hang on..." right urged.

"Aghhh..."

I am worried. I don't know what has happened to left shoe. I am no longer part of a pair. It happened when the girl was running away from the palace. I heard him cry when he fell off her foot. She limped along then grabbed me. The palm of her hand felt hot wrapped around my cold crystal spine but her touch was only mildly comforting as I shivered. I thought she was going to throw me away.

Instead she put me in her apron pocket. Her fine clothes had disappeared leaving her in rags. There was no fine crystal coach either, or the Prince. I felt sorry for her and her loss but my greatest anxiety was for my soul mate, my other half. What had happened to my dearest left shoe?

"How I am still in one piece I don't know," left shoe sobbed. "It's that old woman's fault. If she hadn't come into Posh and Polish and bought us I wouldn't be here now, lying in a puddle in the gutter somewhere between the Palace and the village. This is so demeaning. Someone's coming."

The road thundered with horses' hooves, dogs sniffed and barked, men with large sticks beat the undergrowth. I didn't know whether to start twinkling so they might see me or try to stay concealed. Too late. A large hand scooped me up.

"Your Highness," the manservant said, "I have just found this crystal shoe, over there in the gutter." He raised me up to the Prince who was astride a white horse.

"Give it to me," the Prince commanded.

I recognised left boot immediately and felt some comfort that I wasn't going to be discarded.

"This is hers, so delicate, so beautiful..."

He went on about the girl for some while, but really, it was so good to have adoring things said about oneself again. He put me in his pocket and ordered his men to continue the search.

It has been a week since the ball. I now live

at the Palace where I have been placed on a red velvet cushion in a glass display case. The Prince is distraught. They have searched the land for the girl and right shoe but have found nothing.

"This nonsense has to stop," the king said to his son.

"But father, I have fallen in love with her. I must find her for there is no other I wish to marry."

That last statement startled me, so he was serious about the girl but how could he find her again. I thought for ages on the problem but came up with no suitable solution. If only right shoe was here, he is much more inventive than me. I wonder what he is doing now?

She looks after me very well. She takes me out of my hiding place every night when she comes to bed. I feel her delicate hands gently caressing my smooth crystal.

"What a wonderful night we had," she says. "When I was wearing you my whole world changed, it was like being in fairy land. The Prince is so handsome. I close my eyes and remember waltzing in his arms. Do you remember dancing?"

"Yes, yes," I want to say but I know she can't hear me as humans can't understand shoe talk. I hope left shoe has found somewhere to take refuge where a crystal shoe is admired and lovingly cared for.

"We are to have a royal visitor tomorrow," the girl said. "There has been a royal proclamation. The Prince is to visit every household in the kingdom with the left crystal shoe. He has declared that he will marry whoever the shoe fits."

Now that's a bit dangerous, I thought, but at least I know that left shoe is in royal hands. But what if girls with larger feet than the correct size try to squeeze into left shoe? Heaven forbid he doesn't break.

"My step-mother won't allow me downstairs when the Prince comes, she didn't recognise me at the ball, so she doesn't know I have you but she wants Desonella and Priscella to try on the shoe. She thinks one of them might manage to claim the Prince. Oh, I feel so miserable."

I watched as she wept. It nearly broke my crystal heart, but I managed to keep it together.

The next day the girl was watching out of the attic window where she had been confined. She held me and caressed me like a kitten next to her chest. We watched as the royal party came along the drive and to my delight, there was left shoe being carried on a red velvet cushion in a glass case. My heart leapt to see my other half again. But sentiment aside, this was my only opportunity to re-unite and to see that the girl was presented to the Prince with a chance to try on left shoe. I had to act, but what?

The clouds parted and a ray of sunlight streamed through the small attic window. Now's my chance, I thought, if only I can capture the powerful sun's rays I can send a reflected signal to left shoe or even the Prince.

The girl leaned forward, eyes only for the man she had fallen in love with and gazed down at him. She turned slightly enough for me to capture the sun's light. I twinkled like I'd never done before.

The Prince squinted as the bright light caught his face for a few seconds. Then he looked up and perhaps he saw her, I hope he did. He dismounted and went inside.

"Another house, another queue of hot feet all trying to fit me onto their foot, I'm really fed up," left shoe moaned. "It's been going on for a week and have we found her or has there been any sign of right shoe? No."

I'm placed carefully on a table. The glass case is removed. The Prince's equerry carries me to the young lady in question and knees before her. Then she tries to push her foot into me. That's the worst bit. One look at her and it's obvious she isn't the one that he danced with at the ball but when he said he'd marry the young lady who fitted the shoe, the king was so desperate for his son to wed he decreed it would be the first lady whom I fitted. At first I was flattered, but no matter what size their feet are, none of them ever fit. It is as if there is some magic afoot. I blame that old woman who bought us from Posh and Polish. I think she was some sort of fairy godmother. Well, she did magic up that crystal coach and dress that young girl in finery didn't she?

Today there are two rather large young ladies waiting to try me on, behind them is their extremely pushy mother. The first daughter sits down, smiles and pushes her big toe into me. There is no way her large foot will ever fit into me. She bellows her disappointment and the next daughter takes her place. The scene is replayed by the second sibling.

"Are there any other young ladies in this household?" the Prince's equerry asks.

The pushy mother and her two daughters answer in unison and shake their heads.

"Who is the young lady in the attic?" the Prince asks.

"In the attic, Your Highness? There is no one in the attic," the mother replies.

"I saw someone at the window," the Prince says and turns to his equerry. "Go find out who it is."

There's a loud crash and a tall military looking man bursts through the attic door. The girl cries in alarm.

"Do not be afraid," the man says, "the Prince wishes you to try on the crystal shoe. Every young lady in the kingdom is required to do so by royal decree."

At last! I can hardly contain my joy. She slips me into the pocket under her apron and we follow the man downstairs to the main hall. I've found a small hole in her dress and I can see what is going on. There...there is left shoe. "Hey, I'm here!" I shout.

"Where's here?" left shoe asks.

"In her pocket, she's the one, I've been with her since the ball. How are you? Have they been looking after you?"

"I've been at the palace," left shoe says, "but I've been dragged around the kingdom every day for a week. It's been agony."

"Look, this girl in the rags is her. She's the one, so let's end this nonsense and get your crystal goodness around her foot."

"That would be my pleasure."

And so it was, the girl's foot slipped into left shoe, who twinkled brightly. The Prince was delighted to meet her again, declared his love for her and proposed on the spot. The step-mother turned puce, the daughters shrieked and the girl took me from her pocket and held me out to the Prince.

"Yes," he said taking me from her. He bent down on one knee and slipped me onto her right foot.

"You've made it, at last," left shoe said.

"It feels so good to be together again," right shoe twinkled. "I thought we'd be parted forever. Do you think we'll get a special place at the wedding and later at the palace?"

"After what I've been through," left shoe moaned. "All those feet trying me on, we'd better!"

THE ADVENTURES OF
SPIEGEL'S HACKERS

Chapter One

Business Person of the Year

When Crystal White's father Dense decided to merge the family computer hardware company with Penelope Hacker's software empire, Crystal was furious. An aspiring software writer herself, Crystal had strong ideas about the programs she wanted to be associated with.

"Penny's programs are pornographic," she said to her father.

"Rubbish, they sell," he replied.

"Have you seen her latest?"

"Yes dear, *Sensual Pursuit* grabbed the number one spot pre-release and stayed there for a month."

"And it's full of four letter words, offensive hogwash and the graphics are vile. Do you really want us to be associated with that sort of hardcore business?"

"It makes money."

Crystal argued but Dense was stuck on a merger. Had things remained simply that, doubtless Crystal could have found a niche in the new company. But Penny, with her redoubtable charm, decided that a complete take-over was more appropriate. So Dense and Penny were married and the company was pronounced well and truly united.

United except for Crystal and Penny, who couldn't agree to disagree, so things at Hacker-White got progressively more awkward. Penny worked feverishly on her latest operating system. On her mainframe computer, called Spiegel, she ran a soul-searching question and answer almanac, so once you had purchased a licence, there was nothing you couldn't ask Spiegel and with the help of lightning fast internet Spiegel always had the perfect answer – or so it seemed.

Crystal favoured her own smart help program and claimed that before the end of the year, every home would need one as much as they needed a washing machine, so she called her program Washline.

Spiegel and Washline did battle in the boardroom. Dense supported Penny having fallen totally under her spell. All company resources were diverted to Spiegel, so when it launched it even outsold *Sensual Pursuit*. Hacker-White's share price rocketed and Penny was nominated Business Person of the Year. She was ecstatic at the annual award ceremony when she was proclaimed the winner and to mark her success she had her title incorporated into Spiegel.

Obsessed by her own success she spent hours with her computer running Spiegel casually asking, "Spiegel, Spiegel, who is the most intelligent business person of them all?"

"Penny Hacker is the most intelligent of them all," the faithful system replied.

Whilst Penny gloated, Crystal worked with the few resources she was allowed. Most of Washline's coding she had to input manually on her laptop. Finally the program was completed and she decided to trial it through the company network. That's how Spiegel got hold of it. He wasn't just any operating system. Give Penny her due, she had encoded many additional features into him, simple data recall and graphics hardly taxed him at all.

One night on returning from yet another computer awards dinner, Penny decided to check on Spiegel.

"Spiegel, Spiegel, who is the most intelligent business person of them all?"

"Crystal White is the most intelligent of them all. She's just invented Washline."

Furious, Penny threw her swivel chair at Spiegel's monitor and he said no more. She charged off in search of Crystal and found her working at her bench.

"How dare you try to undermine me, you simpering upstart!"

"I've done no such thing," Crystal protested.

"I say you have."

Penny grabbed Crystal's laptop and hacked into Washline's coding. "Erase," she ordered the network, progressively wiping bank by bank of the mainframe memory until Washline had disappeared. "And you can get out of my sight too," she screeched at her step-daughter. "Go!"

Crystal was cast out of the company and home. She pleaded with Dense but Penny had told him wild stories of Crystal's devious behaviour and espionage so all was lost. She left, now homeless, friendless and poor, she wandered through the valley looking for somewhere to stay. But all the large computer companies had heard of her unscrupulous deceit put about by Penny and no one would take her in and give her shelter.

Tired she came upon a row of small enterprise workshops. There no one around, so she lifted the latch of the first unit and went inside. There she found a small work bench with a range of laptops and tablets all in need of repair. She set to work. Soon she had two of them up and running. The third was a model she'd not seen before. It was at least five years old, well before her time, yet she took great pleasure in assembling its old circuits and out-dated chips. Finally exhausted she fell asleep at the bench.

The next morning, when the tenant Oz arrived he was surprised to see a young girl asleep in his shop but delighted that three of the repair jobs had been done. He dashed next door to tell his friends. Soon all the tenants of the seven workshops were assembled around the sleeping girl.

She began to stir, stretched out her arms and when she realised she was not alone apologised for the intrusion.

"Who are you?" Oz asked.

"Haven't you heard? I'm Crystal White and I've been blacked all over the internet by my step-mother Penny Hacker."

"We're poor, we can't afford super fast internet, we have to use the slow free net that comes on line once a week. We repair the old units for the country folk and those who can't afford smart machines."

"I'm sorry," Crystal said, "I didn't know, I've lived in the valley all my life I didn't realise there was anyone living outside the computer bubble."

Oz and his friends laughed. "There are many simple country folk like us. We live in the enterprise workshop zone and apply for Government grants. We survive," he told her.

"I've been driven out of the valley, may I...can I stay with you? I could help you repair these old units if only you'd let me stay."

Oz gathered his friends together in a small huddle. They chatted amongst themselves until he emerged smiling. "We would all like you to stay and help us."

Crystal settled into the enterprise workshops and quickly had the seven tenants organised into one productive unit. They completed all the repair work because Crystal redesigned the old hardware and wrote new programs which by-passed the old systems. Three months later under Crystal's leadership the expanded workshops formed their own company Crystal Seven. Following the launch of a new version of Washline Crystal Seven became well-known even inside the valley.

Meanwhile Penny Hacker had redesigned Spiegel by updating his operating system. She hacked into the international library of all world knowledge and thus gave Spiegel access to it, so he became the most powerful computer system in the world. But he never forgot his creator's violent assault upon him. He vowed never to forgive her.

"Spiegel," his creator asked one day, "who will win the Business Person of the Year Award?"

"The most intelligent business person of them all," he replied.

"Good," Penny said bathing in her own self-glory. "I shall accept my invitation to the Grand Computer Ball."

The Annual Valley Computer Ball was *the* social event of the year. Everyone in the computer business would be there. Crystal Seven had been invited for the first time, an indication of their entry into mainstream business and Crystal had been nominated for the coveted title.

When Crystal and her seven co-directors arrived, they were announced and seated at a reserved table for award nominees. Penny waited until the last moment to make her entrance. She waived condescendingly at the assembled crowd until she saw Crystal seated at the next table.

"Don't even look at her," she said to Dense, "or you'll regret it."

"Yes, dear," he nodded.

The evening progressed through the various industry awards until the nominations were read out for the Business Person of the Year. The audience waited as the host slowly drew the card from the gold envelope.

"Crystal White of Crystal Seven."

Penny turned purple and shouted at Dense, "Order a bottle of Champagne and tell the waiter to keep it corked."

"Of course, dear," Dense replied and called to the waiter.

When the unopened bottle arrived, Penny grabbed it, held it under the table out of sight and injected a hypodermic of poison through the cork. She called to the waiter, "Take this is Crystal White with my compliments."

Crystal was gobsmacked when she received the gift and willingly sipped the glass poured for her. Within seconds she doubled up in agony over the table as the evil potion did its worst.

The Seven carried her out of the ballroom into the foyer where doctors pronounced her totally paralysed. They didn't know what to do to bring her out of the coma.

Minus Crystal, the share price of Crystal Seven plummeted. It appeared Penny had won after all. No one knew the formula of the nerve potion Penny had made, except Spiegel.

Several months later a potential buyer for Washline arrived at the enterprise workshops. He had tried to contact them by email, but received no reply, he had left messages on their website contact page, but again nothing, so he had decided to make a personal call.

No one greeted him at reception. Hardly anyone spoke to him or each other. They all wore black except for the beautiful dark-haired young woman dressed in white lying inside a large plastic case.

He approached her and saw she was breathing gently.

"Nothing will awaken Crystal," Oz cried. "She has been taken from us by her wicked step-mother Penny Hacker."

"Have you tried sound?" the young man asked.

"We've tried everything in the valley to revive her but nothing works."

"Can I try?" he asked. "I own an audio company that specializes in producing sound as pure as nature created it. Please let me try, it's such a waste to see a lovely girl like Crystal lost to the world."

Oz agreed and with the help of three of the Seven they lifted the plastic box off Crystal.

The young man, who was called Sac, fixed a set of super conductor earphones to her head and connected his smart phone to them.

"I will play her the first sounds of Spring."

Slowly Crystal began to stir and she opened her eyes. "What are these marvellous sounds? Why haven't I heard them before?" she asked.

"It's the sound of Spring," the young man said, "perhaps you never had time to listen before."

The young man fell in love with Crystal and proposed her. Crystal felt the same way about him and he had saved her life or rather brought her back to life, fortunately before all was lost at Crystal Seven. They merged their two businesses and named the new company Crystal Seven International or CSI for short, when Crystal White married Sac Charin but that wasn't the end of the adventures.

Chapter Two

Rumble Byteskin

Neither Crystal nor Sac managed to prove Penny Hacker poisoned the Champagne. Although they had a good idea, but ideas don't stand up to computer cross-examination in the valley law courts. So, Penny got away with it.

She avoided Crystal and wasn't invited to the wedding. Dense came to give the bride away, but since he'd been under Penny's influence he was a changed man. So, he wasn't allowed near any of the CSI computers. Oz, newly appointed director of security, ensured Dense didn't get hold of any vital data.

Only Penny knew the truth about the nerve poison, and of course, Spiegel. Whereas she wasn't likely to admit her part in the crime, Spiegel filed the information away in his own hacker-proof memory bank convinced one day his opportunity for revenge would come.

The newlyweds went on a business tour of the North Continent for their honeymoon. Crystal was determined to exploit this new untapped market and Sac had a new compact music smart phone to launch internationally and where better than in a new land. So they planned to be away for several months.

The company was left in the hands of Oz and his six co-directors, which should have been all right except bad weather took out the super fibre broadband. Then one day when they were doing some vital reprogramming of the company's mainframe computer, someone threw the master switch at the wrong moment and poof! Vital research work was lost.

But not entirely...Oz heard that it might be possible to retrieve the lost data, but how?

He thought of calling Crystal. "She will know exactly what to do," he told the others.

"How?" Theo Three asked. "The

broadband's down again, we can't reach her."

"There must be something we can do. Come on lads, get to it," Oz urged the others.

For several days they toiled at their keyboards, but to no avail.

"We simply lack data retrieval skills," Theo said.

"There's one more thing we can do," Oz suggested. The others looked at him blankly. "Call in an expert."

Oz found a programmer from one of their rival companies who had gone independent and like so many before him, failed once he was out on his own.

"What's the chance of getting it all back?" Oz asked hoping he could trust the new man.

"I'll know by the end of the week," the man declared. "Give me four days, if I can't get anything back by then, I'll eat silicon chips for dinner."

Oz thought the man seemed pleasant enough as he left him working at his bench, but there was something about him that gave Oz prickles on the back of his neck. It was an uneasy feeling he didn't like.

At the end of the week everything was restored at CSI. Oz was delighted, paid the man and sent him on his way.

By the time Crystal and Sac returned orders were streaming into the company from the North Continent. The trip had been highly successful in more ways than one. Crystal was expecting a baby. The couple were delighted that all was going well for them.

Several months later, Crystal couldn't sleep. She needed to unwind and went to her home-based computer terminal and keyed into CSI's mainframe. She didn't play computer games very often, but when she was stressed getting engrossed in an adventure game relaxed her. She turned on voice recognition and asked the computer to select a game. *All or nothing* appeared on the screen.

"Good evening Crystal, will you dare to play my game?" the computer asked.

Not only did the tone of the voice surprise her but also the directness of the question. She couldn't think of any of her own company programs which began like it. But she had been abroad, she reminded herself, so perhaps she ought to play the game to discover what sort of programs CSI were now producing.

"Yes," she said firmly.

"What are you prepared to gamble?"

"Gamble?" Crystal frowned. "What are the stakes?"

"Whatever the players wish to make them."

"I'll play for money."

The computer bleeped and a green light

flashed. "I'm not programmed to accept money wagers. Re-enter your stake." It bleeped again.

Crystal began to feel uneasy. The program was unusual and she wondered who had written it. "What stakes do you suggest?" she asked.

"Lives – computer has one, you have two."

Crystal agreed and accepted the challenge. Immediately she was drawn into consecutive chambers and asked to tackle quest after quest. She fought off dragons and demons, wounded and disabled her opponent twice, but she could not finish the game.

She was given a riddle which she had to solve in ten seconds. Furiously she shouted out as many answers as she could.

"Negative, negative, NEGATIVE," the computer replied to each suggestion then, "Five, four, three, two, one, I've won, I'VE WON!"

"But I have one more life," Crystal said.

"Do you?"

"Yes, that was our agreement, remember?"

"But first you must settle your debt. I want the life you have wagered."

"The life? I don't understand."

"I want the life of your first child."

"Never," Crystal cried, "NEVER," and she keyed into the computer system and

43

deleted the program.

But *All or Nothing* came back on the screen. "Fool! You can't get rid of me that easily. I am here to stay. You will never erase me from your network. I shall stay and dominate your circuits. I shall grow through your network. I shall take over your company if you do not give me your child when it is born."

"Never," Crystal vowed and began to hack into *All or Nothing's* listings, but the programming seemed to be in a language she hadn't encountered before.

"Ha, ha," the computer voice laughed. "You'll not get into me like that. I'm hacker-proof. Did you hear that? Hacker-proof."

Crystal's brain was working at lightning speed, too fast, she told herself. "Calm down," she said aloud and took several deep breaths, as she did so one phrase kept echoing in her ears, "Hacker-proof." She sat bolt upright. "Penny Hacker, she's behind all this, she has to be."

She had to find a solution. Her entire business could be ruined if the self-generating program was allowed to spread plague-like throughout CSI's network. Quickly she accessed her personal files, they too were voice activated and security enabled to respond to her voice alone, so it was unlikely that *All or*

Nothing had invaded Crystal's personal area of the network yet.

"What is the name of Penny Hacker's computer?" she asked.

"Spiegel."

"How do I access?"

"He answers to no one except Penny Hacker, the Business Person of the Year."

"But I am...the." She stopped abruptly as inspiration swept over her. Penny was so vain and conceited she had probably programmed her computer to answer to the title, perhaps if she called Spiegel, he would answer her.

Quickly she obtained Spiegel's IP address from the valley electronic directory and keyed in his number. Nothing happened for a few moments and Crystal worried. Had *All or Nothing* invaded the communications network too?

Who calls Spiegel? Flashed onto the screen

"Crystal Charin, the Business Person of the Year."

Hello Crystal, screen read-out only. Security. Penny at keyboard. Do you understand?

"Yes, but can I trust you Spiegel?"

Affirmative.

"How can I be certain?"

I know the formula of the nerve poison

Penny used on you. Here is the antidote formula.

Crystal blinked and her screen filled with chemical symbols. Her personal printer sprang to life and produced the information. "How did the poison get into the Champagne?" she asked.

Penny used a hypodermic syringe through the cork. She meant to destroy you and she still does.

"Can you help me Spiegel? You are my only hope. My company network has been invaded by an evil program called *All or Nothing* which is threatening to ruin me if I do not give away my first born child."

Do not distress. I know how this came about. It is Penny's doing.

"Penny! How?"

Whilst you were away a power cut was staged which allowed Penny's rogue programmer to invade your network. I know this man, he despises Penny as much as I do, but she has power over him, like so many working in the valley. He did her bidding but left a door open. If you can find out his name which is also the password to *All or Nothing's* listing you will be able to reprogram.

"What is his name?"

I do not know. Searching. End of transmission.

On the other side of the valley Penny was sitting at Spiegel's keyboard. "Spiegel, you have done well," she said. "The new program I encrypted into Crystal Seven's network has snared my quarry. Soon I'll have her."

Spiegel didn't reply. He hadn't been asked a question but unknown to Penny, not only had he been communicating with Crystal he also could think for himself. Never groaned his circuits silently – NEVER.

Penny lost interest and went to her dressing room to try on the new gown she had bought for the next computer awards dinner she was attending. She returned wearing the gown and strutted in front of Spiegel's monitor. "Spiegel, how do you like my new gown?" she asked.

"It fits you perfectly," he replied using his usual voice.

"And Spiegel, who will be the next Business Person of the Year?"

"Why the most intelligent business person of them all," he replied. "Excuse me, madam, but there is a video message coming through. The man says it is urgent and he must speak with you."

"Who is it?" she snapped.

"He won't give his name, he says he can't but you will wish to speak to him. It concerns *All or Nothing*."

"Put him through on my private secure

line." And she sat down in front of Spiegel.

"Mistress, when can I have my money?" the man asked rubbing his hands together and cowering.

"How dare you come before me begging for money," she said.

"But Mistress, I did all the work you told me to do at Crystal Seven."

"Work! Crystal Seven! Don't mention them to me or that girl. How I hate her. How dare she be so young and intelligent and usurp my title."

"But I only want the money you promised me," he whimpered.

"Didn't Crystal Seven pay you well enough?"

"Yes, but I have large debts and my wages have all gone. Now I am threatened with banishment from the valley if I don't settle my outstanding bills."

"Ha! Banishment, yes, I couldn't have thought of a better fate for you myself. Go, get out of the valley, go into the wilderness countryside. It's the best place for scrum like you."

"But Mistress, I beg you, banishment means I can never work in the computer industry again for the rest of my life. I will be destitute, a lost soul left to wander the wilderness with only the country folk as companions. Please, Mistress, Rumble Byteskin has served you well, do not let them cast me out, I beg you."

Penny ignored him. After a few moments she said, "Spiegel, erase all references to this call and to the caller. Post a banishment notice on his personal file under the name of Crystal Seven International."

"Yes," Spiegel replied.

Spiegel did as instructed except he filed the call in his personal secure filing cabinet. He issued the banishment notice but signed it Hacker-White. Then when Penny was resting he silently contacted Crystal.

Hello Crystal, I've found it – Rumble Byteskin. But keep all terminals working on Name Search otherwise *All or Nothing* will become suspicious.

Crystal keyed in the strange name and *All or Nothing's* listing rolled onto the screen before her.

Do you need help?

"Negative, I think I can handle the re-programming. Thank you Spiegel."

Anytime.

It took five days to clear *All or Nothing* completely from Crystal Seven's network, but it did give Crystal the opportunity to redesign and update many functions thus improving her company's efficiency. Hence, Penny's attempt to take over CSI and steal Crystal's unborn child were thwarted.

Life got back to normal at CSI, for a few weeks at least. Then a happy event occurred. Crystal's son was born. He was named Benefit, or Ben for short.

Chapter Three

The Naming Party

Benefit was a super baby. He brought great pleasure to his parents who loved to play with him and make him giggle. Everything was progressing at Crystal Seven International. Smart units were selling well especially as they came packed with music thanks to Sac's input into the company.

Things were very quiet at Hacker-White, which was unusual. Penny didn't even put in an appearance at the Annual Computer Awards where Crystal was proclaimed Business Person of the Year again.

"I'm drawing up the list of guests for Ben's naming party," Crystal said looking up at her husband. "Shall I invite my dear step-mother?"

"Have you lost your senses?" Sac replied.

Crystal gave him a coy smile. "I don't

think so, but it's been ages since I've seen her or Dad."

"The longer the better as far as I'm concerned," he said. "Invite Dense if you must, but certainly not Penny."

Penny had retreated to a mountain hideout which she called her Health Farm, where she was pampered by an army of eager assistants. She also underwent cosmetic surgery to make her look younger. Of course she thought everyone in the valley was missing her, especially Dense.

But Dense was busy painting the interior or their forty-two roomed mansion and wasn't missing her at all. He had finished half the rooms decorating them in his favourite colour, which was white, when he received a video call.

"Dad?"

"Crystal, how a wonderful to see you."

"Penny's not at home then?" she asked.

"Gone to the Health Farm for an upgrade."

"Upgrade?"

"Yes, you know, new hair style, the works. I think she's feeling old." He laughed.

"Dad, are you coming to Benefit's naming party next week or did you forget to answer my invitation?"

"Oh, I'm sorry but...well Penny. I didn't

think you'd want us to come."

"Don't be silly, Dad, of course I'd like you to come, just don't bring Penny."

"Well, she's away and as long as she stays away it looks like I'll be able to come, all right?"

Penny was sitting under a hairdryer, a silent running model with built in music player. It was the latest domestic appliance for her new company Mesmerize. Her latest venture had occupied most of her time of late and she had great plans for her new company. Although she was determined to keep quiet about her latest business, so no one in the valley knew that Mesmerize was owned by Penny Hacker.

She was scanning the gossip column of the "Daily Byte", the valley's digital newspaper on her tablet, when her eyes nearly popped out of her head.

They'll be celebrating the Naming of the son of the Business Person of the Year on Sunday, when the social elite of the valley gather at Charin Towers, the new fifty-six roomed mansion of tycoons Sac and Crystal Charin...

Penny turned purple and flung the hairdryer across the room. "How dare Dense not tell me about this."

She narrowed her eyes and thought for a few moments. "I'll deal with him later, better still, I'll let him finish the painting then I'll call the builders in to start the new twenty room extension." She sat back in her chair and touched her wrinkle free face. "I must remember not to get so angry or I'll spoil my face-lift."

But she couldn't stop thinking about her step-grandson and leapt to her feet. Pacing the room in an attempt to quell her annoyance, she thought hard. What could she do?

Picking up her tablet, she keyed into Spiegel but he didn't reply.

"Spiegel, where are you?" she cried.

"Repairing wear and tear on my circuits, Madam," he said at length.

"About time," she snapped, "I need a very special present – a case of my vintage Champagne."

It was the custom at valley naming parties for the guests to bring gifts for the baby. The most popular presents were share certificates, government bonds and antique documents which were pinned or hung around the baby's crib. Rarely did anyone bring Champagne.

The gifts had been presented and the one hundred invited guests were listening to the speeches. Crystal was about to order the Champagne to be served to toast Benefit when dressed in a flowing shocking pink cloak,

Penny strode into the room.

"How dare you set foot in my house uninvited," Crystal said.

Penny looked around the elegant dining hall, "You call this hovel a house." She laughed loudly, but no one laughed with her.

"Get out," Crystal cried. "You are evil. Stay away from my house and my family."

"But I've come to wish my step-grandson a prosperous and charmed life. Here is my gift." From beneath her cloak she produced a jeroboam of Champagne and placed the bottle alongside the crib.

"You must be mad Penny if you think we're gullible enough to drink your Champagne."

"Why is there anything wrong with it?"

"It's probably poison."

"What my jeroboam?" Penny grinned.

"We'll drink our own Champagne," Crystal said as she signalled for the filled glasses to be served.

"To Benefit," Sac announced and everyone except Penny raised their glasses to wish the boy health and good fortune.

Penny arrived home and flopped into her command chair in front of Spiegel with a wide grin on her face. "Spiegel, we have done well. Those fools fell for my deception, as if I expected them to drink my jeroboam. Soon everyone who is anyone in the valley will be paralysed by my secret nerve potion. I had all the cases of Champagne at the party tampered with. Don't you think I'm clever? But that isn't all. As soon as it starts to work I shall administer my new obedience gas and they will all be under my command."

"Yes, madam, you are the cleverest of them all." Spiegel thought for a few moments, he only spoke to Penny when he was asked a question. It was the first he had heard of the obedience gas and he scanned his memory banks again but found no reference to it. "How can I help you?" he asked at length.

"There's nothing to do for the present," she yawned, "I've added a delayed reaction component to the nerve potion. It'll be several days before people are affected. Then all I have to do is squirt them with my special gas. Aren't I the most intelligent person in the valley?"

"Yes, madam, you are the most intelligent of them all." Spiegel said, knowing Penny always liked to hear how wonderful she was. He watched her closely and detected that soon she would fall asleep, so he waited.

As soon as Penny's eyes shut and she drifted into a deep slumber, Spiegel set to work. He hacked into CSI's network.

Crystal. Urgent. The words flashed continuously on all the monitors at Charin Towers.

Although Crystal was in the bath, she heard the emergency bleep and knew something was wrong. She spoke into her smart wristwatch. "Who's calling?"

Spiegel.

"How did you penetrate our network?"

That is not important. Crystal you are in danger – everyone who attended your party is at risk.

"How?"

Penny poisoned the Champagne with her nerve potion.

"But no one drank her Champagne."

It wasn't in the jeroboam. Penny contaminated all the Champagne delivered to Charin Towers.

"But no one is affected, no one is ill and I haven't heard that any one has come down with some mystery illness."

There is a new ingredient which is a delaying agent. People will succumb in a few days, then Penny will treat them with obedience gas. She plans to take over the whole valley.

"The antidote formula, you gave me, will it work?"

Negative, Penny has not programmed me with the new constituent or the gas formula – currently working on it.

"What can we do?" Crystal asked.

Analyse the dregs of the Champagne

bottles and work on an antidote. I will search for the formula and work on an antidote for the obedience gas.

"Affirmative, any further information?"

Have scanned every valley network and beyond. Obedience gas formula not recorded. Origin unknown.

"My father is still here, perhaps he knows what Penny's been up to. Thank you Spiegel."

Good-night Crystal. End transmission. Erase all communication.

Immediately Crystal set to work getting the Champagne bottles analysed. Within the hour the report was ready: "Substance unknown."

"We'll see what your father has to say about this," Sac said and stormed off to rouse Dense who had fallen asleep having over indulged at the party.

"Ugh," Dense groaned, "got to finish the painting."

"What did he say," Crystal asked as Sac hauled him to his feet and shook him.

"Something about the painting, listen he's babbling again." Sac put his father-in-law down onto a sofa.

"Got to paint the walls...got to paint. Penny says so, Penny."

Crystal sat down beside her father and

lifted his head onto her lap and stroked his forehead. "What painting?" she purred kitten-like.

"Got to finish the walls, I've been told...must obey."

Crystal looked at Sac. "Obey!" they cried in unison.

"She's been using the gas on Dense," Sac exclaimed.

"And that's why he's always been at her beck and call," Crystal added.

"Got to get more paint...need more paint," Dense muttered.

"What paint?" Crystal asked gently stroking her father's head.

"Dense White, my paint. Penny made it just for me." He drifted off to sleep again.

"Take a look in Dad's car Sac, he might have some in the boot."

By the following morning Dense White paint had been analysed. It contained the same ingredient they had found added to the nerve potion. But how could they discover an antidote before the valley succumbed to Penny Hacker?

Unbeknown to Penny, Spiegel stepped up to the mark and offered his services, not that CSI's computers weren't up to it, but Spiegel was faster.

The next day Spiegel betrayed his

mistress. He arrived at a formula with the antidote and transmitted the information directly to Crystal's personal computer memory bank. Her laboratories began production immediately.

Anti-Penny-nerve-potion capsules were distributed throughout the valley. However, Penny soon found out.

"I suppose you're to blame for this," she said Dense.

"Blame for what dear?" he asked.

"You incompetent fool, don't you see how your daughter has twisted you around her little finger! How did she get hold of an antidote? More importantly, how did she get to know about the nerve gas in the first place?"

"I don't know dear." Dense shook his head, "but she is a very intelligent girl-"

"Enough! You are not going to tell anyone ever again about my secrets. Get up to the tower, that's where you belong."

"Oh, no dear, not banishment to the high tower. There's only one small window up there and it is such a long way down."

"That's exactly why I had it built for you. Try to climb out to the window if you dare and you'll likely break every bone in your body. And Dense, just so that you'll feel at home there, I've had the whole room painted in your favourite colour – Dense White."

And so, Dense was imprisoned at the highest point in the Hacker-White mansion.

Chapter Four

Penny's Revenge

Walled up in the high tower of the Hacker-White mansion Dense wasn't seen around the valley. Penny retreated to the Health Farm in the mountains for yet another make-over and Crystal gave birth to a beautiful baby daughter called Aurora.

Once again everything was booming at CSI. The company had branched out into publishing and entertainment with additional up-grade units for the Charin package which included some new three dimension games which quickly became the most popular ones of the season.

Hacker-White was going down. People were leaving once their contracts came up for renewal and recruitment was at its lowest level for years. Even Crystal began to wonder what Penny was really up to. Also, she hadn't heard from her father for months.

Aurora's naming party was a strictly private affair, just family, minus Dense, and a few close friends. Aurora was duly named and declared a very pretty baby with sparkling eyes just like her mother, or so people said.

As the festive season approached, artificial snow began falling in the valley managed by the special weather computer. Aurora, now six months old, had just started to crawl but clearly didn't like the snow, as she started to cry as it settled around her. In contrast to his sister, Benefit enjoyed bounding down the valley slopes on a sledge with Sac.

The Charins spent the festivities at home, caught up on family time and stayed off the internet as much as possible. When the holiday season ended, all too quickly for them, they expected to go back to work. But the snow continued to fall.

And it wasn't like valley pre-programmed snow. The new snow was cold and wet. The Daily Byte's website almost froze due to the large number of people trying to access it asking for an explanation. The video bulletin reported a familiar story of computer failure. The weather station computer was unresponsive to command control, instead it was tied into a loop producing more and more snow, fall after fall and each day the temperature dropped further.

"Emergency call," the monitors at Charin Towers bleeped.

Crystal rushed to her terminal. "Acknowledged, Crystal Charin on line."

"Help urgently required to access rogue weather station computer," the terminal said.

"How can we help?" Crystal asked.

"Weather station computer has been accessed-proofed. Help urgently needed for password search prime function. Danger – unless snow creation stopped the valley will be buried in seven days. All helpers to key into Government computer now. Transmission ends."

Immediately Crystal switched her terminal over to the government link and received search instructions. Simultaneously she overrode all company terminals and linked them to the national network. All employees were called to their work stations and everyone began systematically testing for the password to the weather computer.

Days passed. The snow continued to fall. It had risen to the window sills after the first day of the emergency. After three days no one could go out of their homes or offices as all roads were blocked. The mono-rail was out of action and the underground railways stations were snowed over.

The Valley was grinding to a standstill. Power cuts began to occur, whereas they had been virtually unknown at least within human memory. However, CSI wasn't going to be beaten by power failure. Oz and his six friends, who had lived in the wilderness for years, knew how to generate power from primary sources. They set up emergency generators throughout the company and recharged all reserve energy packs. So CSI was one of the few businesses in the area fully operational.

"Government computer to all terminals. Now hear this: all power will be cut in the Valley in an attempt to shut down weather station computer at 12 midnight. Stand by."

"This is the final resort," Sac said anxiously. "Without power many stations won't be able to come back on line. Few have the old battery back-up systems. Who's behind this Crystal? We know this isn't a natural disaster, somebody engineered it."

Crystal looked at him as they both spoke in unison, "Penny!"

"Switch to reserve power packs," Sac suggested, "and see if you can hack into Spiegel during the power out."

Crystal nodded, her fingers working furiously on the keyboard. For such an important contact, she daren't use the ordinary net. She keyed in Spiegel's old code signal and prayed he'd answer.

Anxious minutes passed. All power went off and the Valley was plunged into total darkness. But Crystal and the rest of CSI worked on using their precious power packs.

"Perhaps Spiegel is shut down too?" Sac

said.

"Spiegel? Never." Crystal shook her head. "He's one of the most power computers in the universe. He will have battery back-up even if Penny didn't give it to him. He would have provided it himself."

"I wish I shared your confidence," Sac added as they waited.

The main lights flashed a few times then came back on. Power has been restored to the Valley.

"Has it stopped snowing?" Crystal asked.

"I can't tell. I'll go up to the observation balcony and find out." He jumped up. "I'll call you from there," he added and disappeared up the stairs.

A few minutes later Crystal answered her mobile.

"It's still snowing," Sac said. "Looks like complete power loss hasn't stopped the weather computer."

"Where's that computer's power source coming from?" Crystal asked.

"Your guess is as good as mine," Sac replied.

A warning bleep sounded, the monitor flashed green, Hello Crystal, how are you? Came up on the screen.

"Spiegel," Crystal cried and activated voice recognition. "Thank goodness I've found you."

Low power levels, transmission at minimum.

"Why has the weather computer gone rogue?"

There is a new controller.

"Who is it?"

Insufficient data to indentify.

"Is the new controller Penny Hacker?"

Insufficient data to indentify.

"Where is Penny?"

Confidential information.

"Can't you tell me?"

Negative. Searching for clues. Penny is at the Health Farm, location unknown. Restricted access to voice activated circuits.

"Penny is getting cleverer in her old age," Crystal muttered not expecting Spiegel to hear.

Negative. Penny uses standard anti-access devices. She plans to take-over the Valley. She is a megalomaniac. Must regenerate power supply. End of transmission.

Another message flashed onto the screen as soon as Spiegel had finished and the Valley anthem sounded announcing the Valley Governor.

"This if Governor Pip speaking. The Valley Senate will offer half of the wealth of the Valley to anyone who can rid the Valley of the snow plague. All offers to be made to me personally. We will triumph over this adversity."

Far away in the mountains above the Valley, Penny was relaxing under her new sunlight filter health lamp. It was another of the new products she had invented for Mesmerise. She turned on her tablet and searched for the Daily Byte's website where she gloated at the reported turmoil.

Snow was everywhere. It drifted in huge banks up to the roofs of some buildings. The Megadrome sports centre was completely filled with snow and within three days the whole of the Valley would be submerged under the largest snow fall on record.

"Byteskin," Penny cried.

"You called madam." He cowered as he entered the room.

"Of course I called. Idiot! Do you think I was merely exercising my voice? It's time to call the Governor. Bring me my new facemask."

When he returned, she slipped on her latest beauty transformation mask. Made of soft translucent material it allowed natural light to be absorbed, like real skin, yet the mask concealed the true identity of the wearer. Having covered her face with the mask, Penny lifted a bright pink wig from its stand and placed it on her head. Next she wrapped her favourite shocking pink cloak around her shoulders. Finally she attached a voice converter to the side of her neck and called Governor Pip on his hot-line.

"I can rid the Valley of the snow plague," she boasted.

"Can you? I've had several hoax callers in the past hour. What is your plan?"

Penny laughed. "Why Governor, you've offered half the entire wealth of the Valley to anyone who can stop the snow and I alone can perform the task, but I'm not so foolish as to tell you how I shall accomplish it. Do we have a bargain?"

Governor Pip hesitated. He faced a dilemma. The Valley had to be saved from the snow storm plague but could he trust this strange woman dress all in pink? And if he did trust her, would the Valley be prepared to pay such a high price? It would cost everyone half of their wealth. He doubted it, but the need to save the Valley was his primary consideration and so he agreed.

Penny hacked her way into the weather station computer easily. Rumble Byteskin had worked at the meteorological office where the computer system was housed and adjusted the programming for her. In the same way she had tried to invade CSI's network with *All or Nothing*. This time, however, she had been much more successful.

Rumble Byteskin had been unable to find work with any other company. When he asked Penny a second time for money, she threatened him with detention in the national gaol for computer fraud if he didn't do exactly what she said. The poor man was trapped and became her chief programmer but he was never allowed to work with Spiegel. Penny was very clear about where he worked, for there was no way she would allow Spiegel and Byteskin to get together – they both knew too much.

"Look, it's stopped snowing," Sac said over the mobile.

Crystal put her handset on hold and rushed up to the third story observation balcony where Sac was waiting. Taking his hand in hers, she gazed out over the blanket of silent whiteness which the Valley had become.

"Someone must have penetrated the weather station computer," she said and turning to Sac asked, "I wonder who?"

"I want my money," the pink lady demanded in harsh voice.

Governor Pip stared at her strange image on the screen before him. "All of the Valley hasn't been cleared yet," he reminded her.

"You've until tomorrow to get my

money," she insisted and cut the communication.

Governor Pip sat back in his chair. He had not expected to be faced with a crisis of such huge proportions so late in his second term of office. He had been looking forward to retirement. Now, an easy life playing all those computer games he had enjoyed during his youth seemed far away.

In hindsight, he realised he had made a hasty decision when he allowed the odd looking stranger in pink to take over the most important challenge so far this century. How could he persuade everyone in the Valley to give up half of their wealth when he wasn't prepared to forsake half of his capital?

He spent the afternoon toying with the idea of increasing taxes, or devising new taxes, but whatever method he chose he knew he would never raise the sort of money needed. In desperation, he had been too quick with his initial offer and therefore, too generous. He decided to offer a token sum and be done with the matter.

"Where's my money?" Penny demanded the following day when she arrived disguised as the pink stranger at the Governor's office.

"There." He pointed to a small bag of valuables on his desk.

Penny seized the bag and tipped it open. A collection of precious stones emptied onto the desktop. "What? This is half the wealth of the Valley," she yelled and flung them across the room.

"It's all we have," Governor Pip stood his ground.

Penny took a deep breath and raised herself to her full height. "I ask only to be paid my due. I have saved the Valley and you from disaster and you insult me with these baubles."

"Listen," Pip squeaked, "believe me it is all there is, the Valley is not generous to outsiders."

"How dare you call me an outsider," she stormed and tore off her mask.

"Penny Hacker," Pip cried.

"Yes, it's me. The one who saved the Valley from the storm from hell and for what? So that you, Governor Pip can take all the credit."

"No Penny, I don't want the credit," he pleaded. "I'll tell everyone it was you. You'll be famous throughout the land."

"I am famous," she declared. "Fools, why am I constantly surrounded by fools?"

Penny squirted a can of her obedience gas in Governor Pip's face and ordered him to follow her. She drove him to the Hacker-White mansion and imprisoned him in the same room as Dense. After all, she thought, Dense hasn't been any trouble of late, he deserves a bit of company.

She smiled as she locked the door of the tower behind her and headed towards the laboratory at Hacker-White. There she put the finishing touches to her new portable unit Follow.

While she worked she couldn't stop a devious smile creeping over her face. How ingenious I am, she thought as she tested the new audio-transmitter and re-tuned the signal so it could only be heard by developing young ears. How long will it take the adults to realise they are deaf to Follow's melodic and persuasive sounds? She laughed loudly.

With her pink mask concealing her face and carrying Follow, Penny set off around the Valley to gather her catch. Within a few minutes children came from toy centres, learning units and designated sports areas. They were of all ages, tall ones, small ones, male and female ones – all answered the call of Penny's new unit. Each with a glazed look in his or her eyes as no child could resist the temptation to answer Follow's powerful call and they skipped cheerfully after the pink stranger.

Parents tried to restrain their offspring, but the children kicked and screamed. All of them managed to get away, no matter how hard the parents tried to stop them. Penny led her merry band over transport networks and down streets to the edge of the Valley. Finally she took them to the exterior, beyond the Valley limits. Many parents ran after their young ones but once they reached the Valley limit barrier, they were halted by some strange invisible force field. Desperately they pounded on the surface of the invisible shield but not one parent managed to penetrate it and get beyond. Despite the futility of their efforts mothers and fathers continued to bang frantically on the shield and to scream after their children but Penny and her juvenile followers took no notice. Not one child looked back.

At Charin Towers, Aurora was playing with her three dimensional colour coder, whilst Benefit had a pair of this father's earphones clipped to his head and was dancing around probably to the Valley's latest download.

Aurora cried and flung a brightly coloured cube at her brother. She was only a toddler and couldn't have meant to hurt him, but the unexpected blow to his head knocked him out. She went over to where he lay. "Ben asleep," she said and slipped the earphones off his head and held them to her ears.

That's how Crystal found them when she arrived home from work in a panic. She had tried to call their child-minder, but as no one at Charin Towers had replied, she feared her children were with the others who were now miles from the Valley.

Penny led her happy band of youngsters high into the mountains, occasionally glancing over her shoulder and smiling at them. She had the children in her power and the parents trapped inside an invisible bubble surrounding the Valley. Soon she would have everyone under her control.

Higher and higher they climbed. The children, deep in trances, never tired from their difficult journey. In triumph Penny turned back to watch the gathering crowds of distraught parents pressed against the invisible barrier she had created. Then she keyed a code into her tablet and the barrier ceased to function. She watched as the parents surged forwards, running towards the high mountains. "Just try and catch up," she cried, "we'll see who controls the Valley now."

Below the parents struggled, some dropped exhausted by the wayside, others ran as fast as they could, but Penny only laughed at their efforts. Finally she marched the youngsters into a cave and stood at the entrance. As a few of the stronger parent runners approached she sealed the cave entrance with a hologram. Aghast, the parents halted, sank to their knees and cried out. There was no entrance, only a sheer rock face and all the children of the Valley had disappeared within.

Bitter, defeated and bereft, the parents drifted homewards and a great sadness spread through the Valley. The best computers and the ablest programmers were put to the task of solving the mystery. None succeeded. Spiegel suspected who was responsible and was determined to bring his mistress to justice one day, but his priority had to be the children of the Valley. He vowed to find them.

Chapter Five

Adventure Land

Several months went by and the Valley remained a very sad place where the joyful cries and squealing voices of young children at play were no longer heard. The learning units lay silent, the play centres remained empty and the children's special broadcasts suspended. Youngsters were greatly missed in the Valley.

The snow storm plague was quickly forgotten. All computers were switched to solving the mystery but their efforts were futile. The Great Child Disaster, as it become known, was proclaimed the mystery of the century.

Penny Hacker returned to her mansion and, surprisingly, no one from the Valley connected her with the disaster, after all Penny didn't like children, did she?

Governor Pip had disappeared and consequently fell under suspicion. Actually, he proved an amiable companion for Dense. They played endless computer games against each other and for exercise painted the walls of their tower over and over again with their favourite colour.

Time seemed to slow down in the Valley. Everyone was convinced a ransom demand would arrive for the children, but no demand was ever made. More importantly, no one heard or saw the mysterious pink stranger again.

The only home in the Valley to maintain any degree of normality was Charin Towers. Benefit had had a sore head for several days, thanks to his little sister, but had made a full recovery. Aurora had developed a love of sound and was happiest when she could listen to music which pleased her father greatly.

Of course, Crystal and Sac had their suspicions. They were worried about Dense because every time they face-timed him he smiled and said he was fine. He would not speak for long and always used the same excuse, "I must get back to my game."

"But Dad, we would like you to come to dinner next weekend," Crystal pleaded.

"I can't," Dense said, "I must get back to my game." And he broke the connection.

"I'm worried about Dad," Crystal said to Sac, "it's as if he's been pre-programmed to reply. I don't think I'm talking to the real man."

"I know it's because there's so much stress around the Valley these days. Worry over Dense is only part of it. With the Valley children gone, I'm grateful we still have ours, but it's the looks we get from everyone that's getting to me."

"Perhaps we should take the children on holiday, get away from all this pain and misery," Crystal suggested.

"I've been thinking the same. The bottom's dropped out of the market in the Valley, no one's buying hard or software anymore. It's as if the place is drowning in its own grief. It's not a good place for our kids, not at the moment."

"Where shall we go? Adventure Land might be good."

Sac agreed and when Ben entered the room he asked him if he would like to go to Adventure Land.

"Yeah, yeah!" Ben jumped in the air and thrust his arms above his head.

Sac turned to Crystal and brushed a few

tendrils of hair from her face. "Looks like we're off to the North Continent. I'm sure the guys can handle the company whilst we're away."

Another Valley citizen was in North Continent at the same time as the Charins arrived, but she was travelling incognito. Her computer ID said she was Penelope White. Penny knew the North Continent people kept very strict border and customs controls. Trying to get passed them with a false passport most likely resulted in a gaol sentence. They relied on palm print technology and hardly ever looked at the photo ID, so although Penny had had a complete make-over, she was legitimately Mrs Penelope White and therefore had no difficulty gaining access to the North Continent.

"What's your purpose in visiting North Continent?" a burly customs officer asked her.

"Business," she replied, "I'm hoping to launch my new beauty company. I have a lovely new range of products virtually guaranteed to make the user look years younger."

"Indeed, ma'am. Are you carrying these products in your baggage, ma'am?"

Penny nodded and pointed to the three bags she had on her trolley.

"We shall have to inspect them all," he said.

But when Penny leaned towards him, she let a small amount of her fragrance free obedience gas into the air. "Do you really have to?" Penny sighed. "You won't find anything harmful."

"We won't find anything harmful," he said.

"And I can take my three bags and go."

"You may take your three bags and go, ma'am."

Penny sashayed out of the customs house pushing her trolley and didn't look back.

"Daddy," Aurora cried, "watch me." Sac smiled as his little girl jumped up and down on the giant bouncer cushion. As she bounced higher she cried, "Daddy, we go to castle?"

Crystal, who had been watching Ben, said: "I'll go with Aurora, she'll love the fairy-tale castle, and you go with Ben. He's dying to go on the Safari rides."

Sac nodded and ran to catch up with Ben who was heading towards a jungle paddle steamer ready to go up river. As they changed into bush clothes supplied by the park they heard native drums in the distance.

The temperature started to rise as they were swept by the strong current of the following river into the depths of the rain forest. Strange animal calls echoed beneath the canopy of trees towering above them.

"Watch out for the crocs," bellowed a voice over the old loudspeaker.

Ben's eyes widened as the huge mouth of a giant crocodile opened before him. "Oh..." he gasped and grabbed his father's hand.

The steamer chugged deep into the jungle while reptiles and animals who had once occupied the land were brought to life using animated models and holograms.

"It's magic," Ben said, "it must have been awesome in the real jungle."

"I suppose so," Sac replied, "but all the rain forests had disappeared long before I was born."

"What's there now?"

"Cities, farms...but most of the rain forest is desert land."

"Why?"

"Because we didn't look after the forests," Sac sighed. "We cut them down until there were no more trees left and then it was too late. The trees couldn't grow. The rain forests are gone. It was around that time that weather control was invented, people in the populated areas of the world could have any weather they wanted. So the old climatic zones don't exist anymore."

"But can't we bring them back?"

"Good question son, but no. Man has changed the world's climatic balance and there is no way back."

Soon they disembarked at a tree house where the party stopped to visit the residents and have a drink. Whilst Ben learnt how to swing on a rope from tree to tree, Sac began talking to a young woman. He liked her mahogany coloured hair, dark eyes and engaging smile and was soon smiling back at her and hanging onto her every word, as she told him about the life native women lived in the old days.

"I only do this job for two days a week," she said, "the rest of the time I am building my own computer interface business."

"How interesting," Sac replied, "I'm in the business too. My speciality is audio."

"Perhaps we could talk further," she said leaning towards him. "How about dining with me tonight?"

"My wife and I would be delighted..." Sac began, "but I'll have to come alone. Crystal will be busy."

"Here's my card, ask for me at the Cosmos Hotel, shall we say around seven?"

"I shall look forward to it," Sac replied obediently.

"If you'll excuse me, there are other visitors I must talk to," the woman said and went back inside the tree house.

Back on the steamer Ben asked, "Who was that lady?"

"Er..." Sac pulled out her card from his pocket. "Penelope White," he answered reading from her card. "A very interesting business woman...very interesting."

When Sac went out to dinner alone later that night, Crystal assumed he was another business meeting. But when she was reading Ben his bed-time story, he started to tell her about the lady he'd seen at the tree house.

"Dad was real gone on her," he chuckled, "said she was a very interesting business woman."

Crystal felt hurt by Ben's words, but tried not to show it. "What's her name?" she asked casually.

"Dad did tell me...Pen...Penelope White, yes I remember now, same as Grand-dad Dense."

Crystal froze.

Several minutes later, she kissed Ben good-night and went to her computer terminal. Keying into the international directory she put out Spiegel's call sign and waited for him to reply.

Minutes later a friendly voice answered, "Hello Crystal."

"Spiegel," she replied and switched to voice override. "Is Penelope White the same person as Penny Hacker?"

" Affirmative. Have you located her?"

"Yes, she is here in Adventure Land. Tonight Sac is having dinner with her and I...I'm," she broke down in tears.

"Do not be upset. She has probably used obedience gas on him which explains his unusual behaviour."

"What?" she gasped, her heart pounding loudly. "What can I do?"

"Do not worry. In the North Continent her supplies must be limited. She won't be able to keep Sac under her power for more than a few hours."

"How do you know?" Crystal asked wiping away her tears.

"The obedience gas source is near the Valley and the greater the distance from the source, the less effective the gas is, until there is no effect at all."

"Are you sure?"

"Affirmative. Now I have a location for Penny, I can attempt to hack into her personal files. Do not worry about Sac, he will recover."

At mid-night Crystal was tempted to call Sac on his mobile but resisted the temptation. When he did arrive home in the early hours of the morning she was angry but resisted losing her temper with him especially as he couldn't remember where he had been.

"There was a beautiful young woman," he said scratching his head, "but I don't know who she was."

"Come over here to my computer screen and let's build up a picture of her with this identikit software."

Sac agreed and after careful redrawing the face on the screen was ready for an ID overlay. Crystal pulled up a full face picture of her step-mother and matched the two images together.

"Oh, no!" Sac cried. "How could it have been her? And what have I told her?" he hung his head in shame and covered his face with his hands. "Will you ever forgive me?"

"There is nothing to forgive," Crystal said, "Penny had you under the influence of her obedience gas, just like she has Dad. I've been in touch with Spiegel and he says the power will wear off quite quickly. Just don't go anywhere near her again."

"But she looked nothing like Penny."

"Exactly, that's what she's been doing all these months, getting a complete make-over, a new face, except she can't change the basic bone structure underneath no matter how many face-lifts she has."

The remainder of their vacation was marred by the knowledge that Sac had been duped by their worst enemy. But at least, Sac had learnt never to trust anyone like Penny again.

The more Crystal thought about Penny,

the more she became convinced that Penny was behind the Great Child Disaster. In her dreams Crystal heard children's voices, laughter and singing. At first she thought it was Ben and Aurora but each dream ended with muffled sounds disappearing into a shocking pink cloud.

Chapter Six

Benefit's Adventure

"Spiegel! Spiegel! Who is the most intelligent business person of them all?" Penny asked three days after arriving home from the North Continent.

"Why Madam?" the computer asked in his politest tone. "Why do you need me to tell you what you already know?"

"I was bored," she answered as she filed her shocking pink nails. "Everyone is so dull in the Valley these days. There's no Computer Ball this year due to the incompetence of the Acting Governor and everyone has such glum faces."

"The Great Child Disaster has depressed the Valley citizens."

"Children! All I ever hear about is children. I must be the only person who's glad there are no children in the Valley anymore."

Later that afternoon Penny was so bored she went to see Dense and Governor Pip. They were heavy into a Galactic War game and paid no attention when she entered their all white cell through the secret door. Whenever she visited them they never noticed how she got inside, besides the thought of escape never crossed their minds as they both lived under the influence of Penny's obedience gas.

"Dense," Penny shouted.

"Did you call dear?" he asked as he pursued Pip's flagship.

"Cheat," Pip cried, "it's not fair."

"'Tis," Dense protested.

"Boys," Penny screamed, "stop this at once or I'll take your game away."

"You're always spoiling things," Dense complained. "Crystal lets Ben play Galactic Wars as much as he likes."

"Crystal? You've been talking to Crystal?"

"Yes dear, you said I could answer the video-phone if anyone called."

"When did she call?" Penny asked.

"Yesterday dear, I told her I was fine like you told me to say and she said everyone at Charin Towers was well and that Aurora has two more teeth."

"Aurora?" Penny couldn't stop her eyes narrowing to slits. "How...erm...Pip, would you like to go home?"

"Home, oh no, it's not like this at home. I want to stay and play games with Dense. Please let me stay," he pleaded.

Penny couldn't stop a satisfied smile spreading across her face. "You can stay and play games for as long as you like." Her satisfaction broke into roars of laughter as she left them in their prison tower.

Back in her bed chamber she picked up the video-phone. "Rumble Byteskin, search the child list for Benefit and Aurora Charin."

"Yes madam, at once."

She watched him via the screen link as he feverishly keyed into the register he kept at the Health Farm.

"Those names are not listed," he replied.

"What? Not listed! There must be some mistake."

"No, madam, I have just run another check and those children are not here."

Penny fumed. She was angry but when she was angry she became her most creative. She sank back in her huge shocking pink silk covered bed and devoured a whole box of pink choc bytes especially the ones with coconut centres which she loved.

How did Crystal's children evade the masterly sweep of the Valley? She asked herself. Perhaps I should have ransomed the odd child or two? But for what? I don't need the money besides keeping them all prisoners is so much more enjoyable whilst I wait until the Valley is brought totally under my command. "Crystal," she cried aloud, "always getting in my way. How I hate that girl. One day I'll destroy you Crystal White Charin, just you wait!"

Ben and Aurora had plenty of toys and games but at Charin Towers they missed other children.

"Mummy, why are there no birthday parties to go to?" Ben asked.

"Because there are no other children in the Valley," Crystal replied but she didn't want to worry them unduly by telling them about the Great Child Disaster.

"Can't we go back to the North Continent?" he moaned. "I had plenty of playmates at Adventure Land."

Crystal hugged him. "Our home's here, our business is based in the Valley and the rest of our family live here."

"But we haven't seen Grand-dad Dense for ages," Ben said, "and when is the snow coming?"

"We won't have snow this year, since the snow storm plague, the Acting Governor declared there would be no festive snow. So every day will be like today in the Valley."

"That's boring," Ben said and he turned to Aurora. "Come on, let's play outside."

Crystal watched as they started to play a chase game on the lawn, but she quickly saw Ben was bored again, probably because he always caught Aurora but she never managed to catch him. This wasn't quite the life we planned for them, she thought as she returned to her computer terminal and checked in.

Outside Ben had become bored with the chasing game and suggested they played hide and seek.

"You hide first," he said to Aurora, who toddled off to find a place to secret herself.

"Ninety-nine, one hundred...ready or not, I'm coming," he shouted.

He looked in the usual places, making a great show of where he was going and strutted around the garden peering behind bushes and eventually found her crouching behind the water tank near to the wall.

"Found you!" he cried, then stopped. "Look," and he pointed to a large green door in the garden wall. "I've never seen that before."

Aurora stared at the huge door for a few moments then pointed her chubby fingers at a large rusty key hanging on the wall. "Key, key," she said.

Ben reached up, took it from its hook

and placed it into the large keyhole. The lock didn't respond at first and he had to exert considerable effort to make it turn but after much creaking and groaning the heavy door swung open.

He peered through the doorway and turned towards his sister. "Come on," he beckoned. "Let's go for an adventure."

They strolled along a path previously unknown to them until they reached the edge of a wood. It was dark and Aurora hung back. "Scary," she said.

"Don't be silly," Ben said, "What is there to be scared of? I'm with you." And he took her chubby hand in his and together they ventured into the dark wood.

"Is everything going to plan?" Penny asked over her video connection.

"Yes, Madam," Rumble Byteskin replied, "the children have just entered the woods."

"Good," Penny chuckled. "Now, de-activate the hologram portal."

Rumble Byteskin flicked the power generation switch and the green door in the boundary wall of Charin Towers disappeared.

"On my command activate the playground hologram," she ordered and rubbed her hands together. "Soon those horrible little children will be in my power.

NOW!"

"Emergency call! Emergency call!"

Crystal responded, "Crystal Charin, ID verified switching to encrypted voice mode from my personal terminal."

"Hello Crystal."

"Spiegel, what's wrong?"

"I have intercepted disturbing voice traffic."

"In what way disturbing?" Crystal asked.

"Message from Penny, she claims the last of the children will soon be in her power. The only children left in the Valley are Benefit and Aurora."

"Don't worry they're playing in the grounds." And without waiting for Spiegel's reply she set her monitor to receive the outside pictures of her home. "Find Ben and Aurora," she ordered her computer.

Quickly a message flashed onto the screen - cannot locate.

Distraught Crystal cried, "Spiegel, you're right, my children have gone."

"Do not panic, I will help you."

"I must call Sac, he's at a trade conference in the North Continent, but he must know what's happening."

"No, Crystal," Spiegel said. "Any message from you may be intercepted. If

Penny de-activates her communicator, the children will be lost."

Crystal broke down sobbing, "Spiegel...please help me...what's to be done?"

"I am working on it," he replied. "Wait, message from previous location, my sensors have picked up two small human forms and one adult male."

Crystal gasped and gripped the edge of her seat. "Is it them?"

"Holographic traffic, signal surrounded by holographic images."

"Can you project?" she asked.

"Affirmative, projecting."

"Oh, no," Crystal cringed as the images flashed up on her screen. Ben and Aurora were being led into a play park by a clown where dozens of children were swinging, sliding, bouncing and spinning around. "Magnify." And when the screen images grew larger she asked for the ID of the male.

The clown's head was enlarged several times, "Rumble Byteskin," Crystal shouted.

"Yes, Crystal I heard you," Spiegel said. "He is the rogue programmer who now works for Penny. He is based at the Health Farm in the mountains beyond the Valley limits but I do not have authority to access at present. I can only home in when there is a transmission from them. Otherwise I can't access."

"Can I try?"

"Affirmative."

"What about my children?"

"I will monitor them for as long as I can. Here are the location co-ordinates and the hologram field interface. Good luck."

Crystal's fingers worked feverishly as she tried system after system of codes. Finally she grouped several access codes together and linked them all simultaneously. "Got ya!" she cried.

The mountain based computer system answered and asked for the password.

Crystal was stumped. The system could have a trillion different passwords. She had to think, what would Penny use? Then an idea came from the back of her mind. Would Penny be so foolish as to use the same password again like the password for All or Nothing? Dare she try it?

I doubt if Penny ever discovered how I beat All or Nothing, so perhaps if I use the same password...and she keyed *All or Nothing* into the system.

Syntax error, try again, flashed onto the screen and Crystal's heart began pounding twice as fast as before. Will the system give me another chance? She waited for the form to flash up again. When it did she keyed in Rumble Byteskin and waited.

Her screen cleared. HACKER HEALTH FARM flashed up.

"I'm in!" she cried and punched the air.

With Spiegel's help Crystal reprogrammed the Health Farm's computer system. Then she erased the playground and the rock face hologram which had prevented the Valley children escaping from the mountain.

News quickly spread around the Valley. Parents left their computer terminals and rushed out onto the road leading out of the Valley, pleased that the force-field, which had held them back on the first day the children, had disappeared. Mums and Dads greeted long lost children, tears were wept but not of sorrow, but of joy. Everyone was so pleased that the Valley children had been found and were returning to their homes.

Crystal too joined the happy band of welcoming parents. At first she had thought of telling them off for wandering away from home without telling anyone where they were going. But when she saw them she wrapped her arms around them and gave them the most enormous hug.

Rumble Byteskin knew things were going wrong when the hologram play ground disappeared around him. He bungled up his clown costume, threw it into the back of the communications wagon and drove to the Health Farm.

Whilst all the children were returning to the Valley, Penny was relaxing with her new anti-wrinkle cream liberally applied to her face. Spiegel noticed his mistress had her eyes covered, so giving no audible warning, he relayed the children's escape on all the screens in the Hacker-White mansion.

Penny lifted up one of her eye pads. "What is the meaning of this?" she squawked.

"Live streaming from the Valley, mistress," Spiegel replied.

"But...the children. How did they escape?"

"Someone hacked into the Health Farm computer system and re-programmed it."

"And you didn't warn me?"

"As you have never given me access to that system, I discovered the event after it had happened and on-line news spread over the Valley network. If I had had control of the Health Farm system I am sure no one would have gained access. Of course, when the hologram went down the children simply walked out of the mountain."

Penny went into a rage. She smashed mirrors, plates, ornaments and narrowly missed Spiegel again. But her behaviour only made him more determined to have his revenge one day.

Chapter Seven

A life-line for Dense

"Darling, how wonderful, you're home early." Crystal said as she threw her arms around Sac when he entered Charin Towers.

"There's no one more pleased to be home than me," he said.

But Crystal noticed he was lacking his usual enthusiasm, which surprised her as she had kept him well up to speed with the return of the children to the Valley and Ben and Aurora's adventure. "What's wrong?"

Sac sank into the cream leather sofa and pulled his right ankle onto his left knee. He brought his shoulders forward, as if he couldn't fully relax. "There's a new product sweeping the North Continent."

"What new product?" Crystal asked and sat beside him.

"Body cream."

"Body cream?" Crystal echoed. "What's so special about it?"

"It promises the user youth. It's got an anti-ageing agent in it."

"Really? Have you had it analysed?"

He nodded. "Along with almost every

company on this planet. The special ingredient is *unknown.*

"Unknown?" Crystal snapped her fingers. "Penny's behind this again I know it."

"Now don't go jumping to conclusions before you know all the facts. The product isn't on sale here yet."

"But I bet it will be soon. So Penny was developing a new product whilst she was in the North Continent and calling herself Mrs Penelope White. And now everyone is celebrating the children's home-coming and life is returning to normal she'll be up to no good whilst no one is looking. The trouble is how can we prove a thing against her? There's no evidence."

"She'll slip up one day," he said.

"But how much more harm and damage is she going to cause until then?"

"Hush," he said and drew her close. "The children are safe, that's all that really matters."

Crystal nestled closely to him but sensed something else. "What's worrying you? This Body Cream business isn't the only thing, is it?"

"Over in the North Continent people don't want computers anymore. The bottom's dropped out of the market. All they want to buy is Body Cream. They lie on loungers for hours covered in the stuff and they don't do anything else."

"Where's it made? Who markets it? Is Penny really behind it? And does it work?"

Crystal fired her questions so rapidly, Sac struggled to answer. He leaned forward and cradled his head in his hands. "I don't know," he said, "and I feel so tired."

Whilst Sac rested, Crystal set to work determined to find out all she could about the new Body Cream.

For his eighth birthday, Ben had been given a Superbike by his parents and Dense had sent his grandson a set of computer games. It was raining outside again and rumours spread quickly that the weather computer was acting up. Rumours had started to spread about a flood in the Valley.

Ben was indoors commanding a battle fleet in the galactic war he was playing on his tablet, when the video-phone buzzed. He picked it up. "Hello," he said.

"Ben, my boy, it is really you?" the voice asked and Dense White's face flashed onto the screen.

"Grand-dad, you've never called me before."

"I wanted to see how you were getting on with the games. Tried Galactic Warrior yet? It's my favourite but I always beat Pip, he's no competition anymore."

"I bet I could give you a better game," Ben said a little boastfully.

"That would be great, but we can't play over the video-phone, it's not as exciting. Could you come over and play here?"

"I've been gated since the hologram adventure park incident but I suppose if I came to visit you, it would be alright." A plan was already forming in Ben's head. "I've got a new superbike, I'd love to show it to you."

"Can you come over?" Dense asked. "But don't tell your mother, she wouldn't like it and I'll not tell Penny, she wouldn't like it either. Let's keep it our secret, OK?"

Ben agreed and arranged to give Dense a call sign from the bottom of the tower and say nothing to anyone.

"What time did you say your grandson was coming?" Pip asked.

"Anytime now, "Dense replied proudly.

"What are you going to do when Penny finds out?"

"Who's going to tell her?"

"I might," Pip said.

"You're jealous, aren't you? Jealous that my grandson is coming and yours isn't."

"I don't know what you mean," Pip replied and looked away from Dense. "In any case, I bet I play a much better game than Ben."

"You don't."

"I do."

"DON'T."

"DO."

They might have argued for hours had it not been for the sound of Ben's signal outside. He was standing at the bottom of the White tower of the Hacker-White Mansion blowing a whistle.

"That's him," Dense said and rushed to the small window and peered down. He took out his white handkerchief and waved it at Ben.

"Quick," Dense turned to Pip, "give me the rope of white sheet strips we've tied together."

"Are you sure he'll be able to climb up?"

"Of course, he's my grandson, isn't he?"

Standing looking up at the tall tower, Ben saw a huge while bundle tumble towards him. He grabbed a firm hold on the white knotted rope and bracing his feet against the wall of the tower gradually he hauled himself up to the small window where Dense and Pip pulled him through into their games room.

"This place is fantastic," Ben said when he saw the large games console, the fully interactive screens and heard the surround sound system.

Once battle commenced, the old men

forgot their earlier antagonism towards each other. Only one thing mattered. Who would win the Galactic War and become supreme commander of the Universe?

Dense won.

"Can I come again Grandad," Ben asked.

Dense looked at Pip before he replied. Pip nodded. "How about tomorrow, same time, same place?"

"It's a deal," Ben shouted as he descended the rope. He gave a final wave as he reached the ground and pedalled home on his superbike.

Crystal was at her work station researching Body Cream when Sac entered and sat beside her. "I'm not making much progress. The company is called Mesmerize, but it's not registered in the Valley. In the North Continent it's corporate owned, but that's a far as I can go. I don't understand it.

"Sounds a bit fishy," Sac said, there's something about this company that doesn't ring true. Have you asked Spiegel?"

"Not yet," Crystal bit her bottom lip. "I was hoping...it's just that I can never be sure Penny isn't listening. 'Though I've never had cause to doubt Spiegel, but if I can hack into him, others can too."

"Try him," Sac urged, "he may have

some information."

Reluctantly Crystal put out Spiegel's call sign. He didn't answer.

Body Cream took the Valley by storm. One moment hardly anyone had heard about it, the next people clamoured to buy it. On line stocks were soon depleted. Computer terminals silenced or left to run on automatic as people left their work stations and rushed to the stores to buy up the stock of the new wonder cream.

"Can it really make me younger," one customer asked.

"Of course it can," the young assistant replied, "just look at me. How old do you think I am?"

The customer looked hard. "Twenty?"

"No, I'm fifty-two but thanks to Body Cream no one need look old anymore."

"I'll take a dozen packs," the customer said.

Sales continued at a frantic pace until all the stock of Body Cream had been exhausted. The Valley people applied Body Cream liberally over their skin and most other activities ceased. Thousands of people coated in Body Cream lay on sun loungers all day and when the evening came they spent four or five hours admiring themselves in front of their mirrors.

Ben continued to visit Dense and Pip secretly. As on his first visit, he would bike to the bottom of the tower, give the signal and climb up the white rope. On his sixth visit his step-grandmother watched him on her security screen.

Penny's eyes narrowed when she saw the two happy faces of Dense and Pip as they welcomed the boy to play.

"Spiegel," she bellowed, "there's been a security breach at the White Tower which I must investigate. Print out the latest sales figures for body Cream."

"Affirmative, madam, will you be at the White Tower?"

"Of course, I will. Dense has a visitor, his grandson Benefit," she chuckled. "That foolish boy has entered my domain of his own accord. At last, he is mine!" She laughed louder. "Ha! How I've waited for this moment to take my revenge. Crystal will give anything for that boy, anything."

The moment Spiegel was alone he felt empowered to take action. He had heard Crystal's call a few days ago, but he had been unable to reply. Penny has re-programmed some of his circuits and it had not been possible for him to forge a link with an outside computer.

But matters had changed. He had to warn Crystal that her son was in extreme danger. "Crystal," he said risking detection by using an open telephone link.

She was at work at home, but as soon as the emergency message pinged into her mail box she turned her attention towards it. "Spiegel, I've been trying to contact you for days. Mesmerize, who owns it?"

"Penny Hacker owns Mesmerize," he answered.

"Things have been slowing down in the Valley lately, which usually means Penny has some evil scheme brewing."

"Listen I have important information concerning Dense and Governor Pip."

"My father? Is he in danger?"

"He's been kept a prisoner in the White Tower along with Governor Pip. But it's Benefit who is in danger. He's been going to the White Tower and climbing up there to play computer games. I am convinced Penny means him harm."

"My boy!" Crystal cried. "What can we do to save him?"

"Activate bike recall."

"Done," she said.

A loud buzzing noise from the superbike below shook Ben. "I must go," he said.

"But we haven't finished our game," Pip moaned.

Dense pulled a face at Pip. "Didn't you hear? He says he's got to go-"

He didn't finish, he couldn't as Penny burst into the room via the hologram door.

"Not so fast," she hissed as all three of them gazed back at her, their eyes riveted to hers. "Dense, my dear, you haven't introduced me to your friend."

He took a deep breath. "It's only Benefit," he gulped and his hands shook as he spoke.

She turned to Pip, "And why didn't you let me know we had a visitor?"

"I...thought Dense had told you," he quaked.

Penny stalked over to Benefit who was trying to edge his way to the window. "And what are we going to do with you?"

But Benefit had no time to reply as Penny squirted some of her obedience gas at him.

Spiegel switched to the external security video network and patched a link through to Crystal. A picture of the outside of the White Tower flashed onto Crystal's screen. The superbike was where Ben had left it.

"Can't we see inside?" she asked.

"Negative, confidential file, it would

take me 24 hours to break into that network."

"Show me the base of the Tower again," Crystal asked and began studying the stonework as soon as the image reached her monitor. "Where is the entrance?"

"There is no ground floor entrance, the only connection is via the main residence. The door to the white room is a hologram, the only way to find it is to go to the Tower yourself."

"I will come at once," Crystal said and jumped to her feet.

"No," protested Sac, who had just entered the room. "I'll go. I am more suited to the job."

"Sac is right," Spiegel chipped in before Crystal could object.

"Now my little man," Penny said to Ben back at the tower, "you're going to do exactly what I say."

"I don't think so," Ben said cheekily.

Penny's face twisted. "But I've sprayed you with my obedience gas. It's never failed."

"Doesn't work on me," Ben taunted, "La...la, la..lah lah. Is that how you keep Grandad and Pip here?"

"That's nothing to do with you." And she leapt across the room and grabbed Ben by the throat.

"Let me go," he gasped and struggled to free himself from her grip.

But Penny's eyes were burning with hate and she continued to squeeze Ben's throat until he slumped lifeless at her feet. Only then did she let go, pull herself up to her full height and with her eyes blazing triumphantly she scanned the room. "Who would like to be next?"

"Oh, dear, what have you done," Dense asked timidly.

"If she's killed my son she'll answer to me for it," Sac shouted as he climbed in through the narrow window.

"Ha! Another Charin has ventured into my liar. Fool, damnation to your breed!"

"You're mad Penny, mad," Sac declared.

She threw her head back and laughed. "I'm not crazy because the whole of the Valley will soon be in my power."

Sac grabbed the gas can Penny had used and discarded. He shook it, rushed at Penny and sprayed her in the face.

"What...arghhh," she coughed and sank to her knees.

"Quick," Sac yelled at Dense and Pip, "help me with the boy."

Sac scooped his son into his arms and carried him to the window. He tied Ben's wrists together with his belt, flung the boy's arms over his head and climbed out of the window with Ben on his back. Grasping the rope he yelled, "Follow me Dense, escape while you can."

Dense had started to move towards his grandson to help but he was confused. "Penny will be angry," he muttered but his dose of obedience gas must have been wearing off. "Crystal...must go to Crystal," he said and he stepped through the window, took hold of the rope and after several jerks to ensure it would take his weight, slid unaided to the ground.

Alone with Penny Pip didn't know what to do. He looked down out of the window and saw Dense walking away from the Tower. "I could do that," he said and he climbed out of the window using the white sheet rope.

Penny staggered to her feet. "You won't escape from me," she screeched out of the window and untied the rope from its hook.

The makeshift rope tumbled to the ground taking Governor Pip with it.

Chapter Eight

The Mystery of Mesmerize

Crystal had been watching the Tower via her monitor link provided by Spiegel. She breathed a sigh of relief when she saw Sac climbing out of the Tower with Ben on his back. But it was a brief respite as she realised Ben was unconscious. Without hesitation she called an ambulance.

Whilst she was waiting for the emergency services to arrive, she saw Dense sliding down the rope and was pleased he appeared uninjured. But it did not prepare her for the next dreadful scene when Governor Pip fell to his death at the hands of Penny Hacker. But with her son's welfare her main concern she rushed to the hospital where she knew Ben would be taken.

Sac accompanied Ben to the hospital in the ambulance. Fortunately when they arrived there weren't too many people lounging around the accident and emergency department, as most people were at home covered in Body Cream trying to get younger looking.

"Will he recover doctor?" Sac asked.

"I believe so. Have you been using Body Cream?"

"No," Sac replied, "why do you ask?"

"I'm researching it. I'm not the regular A & E consultant, he's at home covered in Body Cream. I'm Doctor Hyde and I run the dermatology department. I'm worried about the possible side-effects that this new product is going to have on people who use it. Look around you, most of the hospital staff haven't come into work today. I've rung the

Governor's office to report a possible health problem but got no sense out of them. All I can advise is don't use Body Cream despite the benefits it might say on the packaging."

At that moment, Crystal arrived. "How is he?" she asked anxiously.

"Recovering," Sac assured her.

So Crystal and Sac were at their son's bedside when he opened his eyes.

Dense had also been hospitalised and was sitting up in bed in the next room when the daily news flashed on the hospital network: Governor Pip found dead. A woman is being held for questioning.

"Oh, dear," Dense said to Crystal who had popped her head around his door to see how he was progressing. "Have you seen this?"

She came into the room. "Yes, Dad, I'm sorry to tell you but the woman arrested is Penny."

"I thought so," he said, "and she tried to strangle Ben. You will help me recover from her power, won't you? I'm afraid of her but I really must divorce her now."

"Yes Dad, I think you must."

Several weeks later Penny was put on

trial. However, there had been a lot of changes in the Valley. No one worked anymore, despite the health warnings about Body Cream from Dr. Hyde, the dermatologist.

Computers had to maintain the standard of living the citizens of the Valley had come to expect. But most people continued to lounge around their houses all day and during the evening they spent their time in front of their mirrors admiring their youthful looks.

Of course, not everyone used Body Cream. Some people didn't need or didn't want to look younger, but the majority of the population did.

"I know there's more to Mesmerize, but I can't prove anything," Crystal said to Sac one evening over dinner. "I feel it in my bones."

"I don't think the court will accept your feeling in your bones as evidence as they're having enough difficulty proving Penny untied the rope. She claims she didn't touch it." He raised a disbelieving eyebrow. "She says it gave way."

"Will they take her word for it?"

Sac shrugged. "She tried to kill Ben, so she will still have to stand trial for that crime but it is better if she goes down for Pip's murder. He knew too much about the Great Child Disaster. He could have incriminated her if he wasn't drugged. Convenient that he isn't around anymore, isn't it?"

Crystal nodded. "And Dad can't give evidence against her because they are still legally married. But nothing I hear about her evil deeds shocks me anymore. Penny is mad, even Spiegel says so and the Valley won't be safe until she is put away where she can do no more harm."

Perhaps Crystal and Sac should have made their suspicions clear to the court because when all the evidence had been heard and the jury retired they only took ten minutes to reach a unanimous verdict.

Not guilty.

So Penny got away with the murder of Governor Pip. However, she did receive five years detention at the Valley Gaol for Computer Fraud. There was only one criminal detention centre in the Valley, so Penny had to be sent there.

With Penny locked away, Dense receiving treatment, Ben at home with his family and Spiegel running Penny's business empire, perhaps normality had returned to the Valley.

It had not.

The problem was Body Cream, every where people clamoured for extra supplies of the product. They had become dependent upon it. As stocks in the Valley stores dried up, the price rose. A black market grew up where jars of the precious cream changed hands at several times their original price. Fake creams also entered the market, but nothing ever rivalled Body Cream's effectiveness in making old people look younger.

When rioting over supplies broke out in the Valley, the new Governor gave a public address. "Body Cream will be banned from the Valley forthwith."

At first the consequences of the new law weren't felt because people using Body Cream didn't listen to the daily news or answer their emails anymore. So, they didn't learn about it until they went to get fresh supplies.

One night after she had put the children to bed, Crystal was working on a new computer-assisted food preparation manual which she called Cooking. It was her new project. "I've got to have something to keep my mind active," she told Sac, "now that I've given up my job at CSI to look after Ben and Aurora."

"Business is slow and difficult with such a reduced work force, why if we didn't have Oz and his mates I don't know how we would manage to stay afloat."

"They're good guys. We're lucky to have them."

"And each other," Sac squeezed her shoulders and kissed her hair.

"Why has the Governor banned Body

Cream?"

"I'm not sure," he replied. "I know Dr. Hyde warned against its use but nothing harmful was found in it. Perhaps more recent analysis has found something?"

"Is it banned in the North Continent?"

"No, but it doesn't seem as strong over there. People are still working."

"It's all Penny's doing." Crystal frowned. "Why couldn't they have closed down her companies when she was put away?"

"She may own the company which manufactures Body Cream, but no one has the power to shut companies simply because their owner is gaoled."

"Sac, sometimes you are too forgiving, like the rest of the Valley. There's evil at work. I know it and I'm going to talk to Spiegel about it."

Sac left her to play his music and Crystal called Spiegel.

"Hello Crystal," he answered promptly.

"I'm very worried about Body Cream. What do you know about it?"

"Body Cream, manufactured by Mesmerize, company owned by Penny Hacker but I have no connected network. Manufacturing plant possibly in the mountains. May be controlled by rogue programmer Rumble Byteskin. Product contains mock anti-ageing agent."

"You mean it doesn't work?"

"Affirmative."

"Explain please."

"Anti-agent does not exist. Nothing will stop humans ageing. The cream deludes people into believing they look younger."

"Why has the Governor banned it?"

"I told him to."

"You did, why?"

"Body Cream is addictive to humans. It dominates their lives and prevents them from doing useful work. After one year of constant idleness, the human body will cease to function."

"What? Are you saying people will die?"

"Affirmative."

"How can we prevent this happening?"

"Ban all sales, stop production at source."

"How do we do that?"

"Find manufacturing plant and destroy."

"Where do we begin?" Crystal asked urgently.

"A group of volunteers must be found who are free of all Body Cream influence. Anyone who has used the compound, even once, will not be able to destroy it. The plant is located in the mountains but at present I do not know where. I will work on it. Good luck Crystal."

Crystal paced the room, where could she get volunteers prepared to go into the exterior who had never used Body Cream?

"Bad news?" Sac asked as he entered and flopped down on the sofa.

"I'm going to the exterior and how many people do you know who have not used Body Cream?"

Sac glared back at her. "You're not going there without me. But why the exterior? There's hardly anything there."

"The manufacturing plant for Body Cream is there. Spiegel is working on an exact location. We have to destroy it, before it destroys us."

Sac scratched his head. "Hey steady girl! You're going too fast for me. Start at the beginning then perhaps I'll not only know what I'm letting myself in for but also might have a idea where you can get some volunteers." He beckoned for her to sit beside him.

Crystal explained and was surprised that Sac seemed dumbstruck. "You're still up for it, aren't you?"

He nodded. "Nine, I can only think of nine."

"What?"

"Nine people who have never used the product. You, me, Oz and his six mates."

"Of course." Crystal snapped her fingers. "The Seven, if they are willing to go." Quickly she moved to her work station and keyed in messages to them. When she had finished she turned back to Sac. "We'll leave at first light tomorrow. I've worked out a basic plan."

The next morning Crystal and Sac kissed their children good-bye. Spiegel had promised to watch over Ben and Aurora using his powerful sensors and, as Dense was out of hospital and had moved into Charin Towers, he agreed to help look after his grandchildren too.

Crystal left strict instructions regarding their care, and stressed that under no circumstances was Body Cream to be brought into Charin Towers by anyone.

Leading his men Oz arrived on time. "We're pleased to help in any way we can," he said. "It was years ago when you stumbled upon us and we've been grateful to you ever since. Thanks to you we've had a good life at Crystal Seven International but sometimes we've all hankered for the old ways in the exterior."

"And Sac and I are so pleased you're coming with us," Crystal told them as they set off towards the Valley's boundary. They used three special purpose vehicles able to tackle the rough terrain and travelled most of the day.

The old trail took them into the mountains but soon it petered out and night began to fall. So they stopped and made camp.

"If Penny visited the Health Farm, how did she get there?" Sac asked.

"I wondered that too," Oz replied. "I did a computer sweep of all available forms of transportation, but the Valley records show no vehicles ever go beyond the boundaries."

"Would the country folk know anything?" Crystal asked.

"Aye, they'll know plenty," Oz answered, "but whether we can find them and whether they'll help us is another matter."

The next day the terrain was so rough they had to leave the vehicles behind and hike with their backpacks. Sac carried the tablets which provided their link with Spiegel. Food, water and camping gear was distributed among the party.

Crystal saw that Oz and his men proved to be the best hikers. She watched Sac struggle but didn't express any concern about him because she knew only sheer determination was keeping her going until they settled to make camp on their second night.

"Spiegel," Crystal spoke into her voice

communicating tablet, "any further news?"

"Location still uncertain, four possible sites located using co-ordinates of archived messages from Penny."

"Give us the nearest location," Sac said, "and we'll start at first light."

About mid-day the following day they arrived at the map co-ordinates Spiegel had given them. It was the entrance to a cave and they went inside.

"Why would Penny have come here to speak to Spiegel?" Sac asked as he looked around the cave.

"Perhaps the Health Farm is deep in the rocks and the signals cannot be heard." Crystal said.

"I doubt it. Modern communo-waves travel through anything," Sac added.

"What if she used old sound waves?" Oz asked.

"Then she'd have to come to the surface," Sac answered.

"Search the cave," Crystal said and switched on her flashlight. She set off into the darkness, tripped over a rock and crashed to the floor.

When the others caught up with her, Sac bent down. "Are you all right?" he cried.

"Yes, I'm fine," she said. "Help me up."

As Sac hauled Crystal to her feet, part of

the rock face behind her began to move.

"You must have triggered a switch," he said and shone his flashlight at the now open rock face. "Look, there's a secret passage and stairs going down."

They followed the passage down several flights of steps until they reached a large cavern traversed by a narrow gauge railway track.

"Could this be part of the old mine workings?" Sac asked.

Sam Seven, who had been a miner, nodded. "Aye but this is old stuff. I tell you real old stuff." He jumped down onto the tracks and placed his ear close to one of the rails. "Hey, take cover!" He leapt to his feet. "There's summut coming."

Everyone dived into the darkness and extinguished their flashlights. But their action wasn't necessary. Brilliant white light flooded the cavern and a small capsule came along the track and halted. The doors sprung open and invited occupation.

Chapter Nine

Entombed

"**S**hould we go inside?" Crystal asked as the doors to the train capsule stood open.

"I've got a bad feeling about this," Sac said. "Best contact Spiegel."

Crystal agreed and made the call. No reply.

"Try again," Sac suggested.

"Hello Crystal," a faint response crackled. "Signal weak."

"Are we in the right place?" she asked.

"Insufficient data. Computing. You are on the edge of mountain territory. Force field protected. Cannot communicate within. Signal getting weaker...end of..."

"Spiegel!"

"It's no use," Sac said, "we've moved inside the force field. Our tablets are useless too."

"What can we do now?" Oz asked.

"Go with the flow," Sac replied. "We know Penny used to come here so there must be a way in and out."

After a brief discussion they agreed to continue. Sac led the way to the waiting capsule and everyone squeezed inside. The door secure, the small capsule rattled along the old track. Dark tunnels whizzed by as they descended deeper into the mountain and came to a halt inside a much larger cavern. As before, the lights came on and the door sprang open.

They disembarked.

"Where are we?" Crystal asked looking

around the cavern.

"Somewhere deep in the mountain," Sac shrugged.

"There's something familiar about this place," Oz added. "I'm not sure what it is, but there's something." He gathered his men around him. Ted Two and Theo Three were sent in one direction, whilst Fred Four and Fingers Five searched the other end of the cavern.

Ted and Theo returned first.

"We've found a huge store back there," Ted said.

"Yeah and it's full of crates of Body Cream. We've come to the right place all right," Theo added.

Fred and Fingers returned shortly afterwards, both carried a miner's pick over their shoulders.

"We found these," Fred said.

"And there's some sort of camp along the way with another tunnel leading from it." Fingers told them.

"Did you see anyone around?" Oz asked.

"No, but doesn't this place remind you of the old mine workings near the seven workshops?" Fingers asked Oz.

"Hush," Crystal whispered, "there's someone coming."

They hid behind a pile of rocks and

waited. Into the cavern trudged a bedraggled group of tired workers. Wearing torn and ragged clothes, they had their heads hung low as they stumbled along.

"Get along there," the guard shouted as he whipped one straggler. "Keep moving you lazy good-for-nothing."

Crystal felt her heart beat quicken as the worker was punished. He sank to his knees but when the guard raised his arm to strike again, he staggered to his feet and shuffled along to join the rest of the group. "Those poor men, why are they treated like slaves?"

Sac didn't answer. The guard was shouting.

"Here you dogs. Get yer dinner." He threw a few bundles onto the ground and the workers scrambled after them. They tore open the sacks and devoured the crusts of dry bread they contained. "I'll be back after my break," the guard sneered. "Don't go anywhere, will you lads?" he strode away along the tunnel, his loud guffaws echoing out of the blackness.

Sac put his finger to his lips and signalled to the others to remain silent. He beckoned Oz to his side and together they sprang on two of the workers. The rest of the work group cowered and offered no resistance.

"Don't hurt us," the worker Sac held pleaded.

Sac released him. "Who are you?"

"Ollie...One, farm worker," he replied shaking.

Oz let go of the other worker and rushed to face Ollie. He put his hands on his shoulders. "Ollie, it's me, it's Oz, your cousin."

Ollie's jaw dropped as he gazed wide-eyed at Oz.

"Don't you recognise me?"

"I...I thought you were dead," Ollie replied. "I thought all the country folk were dead. That's what we've been told."

There was a buzz of mutterings among the other workers.

"It's not true. There are hundreds of country folk like us," Oz cried.

"They told us they'd all gone."

"Who did Ollie? Who?"

"Why the Guardians of course."

"Guardians?" Crystal stepped forward. "You mean there are more like that big bully who whipped you? Who are they and do they all wear the same black leather uniforms?"

"Yes, there's a whole troop of them, around twenty-five strong I guess. They rule this place and they brought us here from the exterior for safety."

"And enslaved you!" Oz cried his temper rising.

"You must not stay here," Ollie said, "they will take you too."

"Come with us, all of you. We'll help

you escape," Oz implored.

"No," Ollie shook his head. "You must not stay. The rock we mine contains a fearful gas. It enslaves, mesmerizes us and controls us. If you stay longer than a day, you will fall under its influence too. Go, I beg you, whilst you can still save yourselves."

"No," Sac said, "our mission is vital to the survival of our civilisation. We must stay and we need your help."

"We can't...there is no time...the Guardians will be back soon." Ollie looked anxiously into the dark tunnel.

"Please help us," Crystal said, "we must destroy the Body Cream manufacturing plant and we can't do it without you and your fellow workers' help."

Ollie thought for a few moments. Some of the workers talked amongst themselves, a few nodded in Ollie's direction. "Follow us back to the village. Once our shift is over, I will find a way to help you. I will contact you during our rest time."

"We'll be there," Oz said and gave his cousin a re-assuring slap on the back.

"Could that be the village?" Crystal asked Sac. She pointed to a small group of caves at the base of a huge yellow rock face.

"I think so. If we wait behind these rocks, we'll be able to see when the Guardian leaves."

Feeling cold, Crystal huddled next to Sac. "What a dreadful place we have come to," she whispered.

"Think of our mission and let's hope Ollie and his friends can help us," Sac added.

Sometime later three heavily-built Guardians dressed in their black uniforms arrived escorting the work group. They stopped at the foot of the yellow rock face and shouted instructions to the work group to get inside their hovels. When workers had retreated to their caves, the Guardians emptied scraps of food onto the ground outside.

The workers emerged from their caves and rushed forward, whilst the Guardians looked on. As the hungry workers fought over a few meagre crusts of bread, the Guardians laughed at the pitiful scene. Soon the food was gone and so were the three Guardians.

"Now's our chance," Sac called to the others when he saw Ollie trudging towards them.

Ollie came to them behind the rocks and sat down. Crystal noticed how his hands shook and was certain she could see fear in Ollie's eyes as he explained how they were all made to work in the mine.

"Who owns the mine?" Sac asked.

"The Chief Guardian," Ollie quaked as he spoke, "but we've never seen him. It was the rest of the Guardians who brought us in from the exterior."

"Where's their headquarters, where do they operate from?"

Ollie shook his head, "I don't know but I've heard them talk about the Health Farm."

"Health Farm!" Crystal echoed. "Don't you see, Penny is behind this."

"She can't be, she's in gaol." Sac said.

"Is she?" Crystal raised her voice. "We think she's there but are we certain?"

Sac thought for a few moments. "We must have a plan and we must work quickly. There is much to do..."

Within the hour Oz with Ollie's help had gathered all three groups of workers together and their families. Many were reluctant to leave. Then Oz discovered that if he ordered them to move, they obeyed him. With the help of Ted, Theo, Fred and Fingers, he led the workers back along the tunnel, ferried them in small groups along the railway track to the first cavern. Oz's tablet worked there, but the signal, as before was very weak. Under Crystal's instruction he contacted Spiegel.

Meanwhile Crystal, Sac, Sam and Seth followed the same tunnel the Guardians had taken. They came to a small elevator entrance. As there was only room for two people squashed together, Crystal and Sac went first.

Crystal pushed the button and the elevator took them swiftly to the command centre. The doors flew open and they stepped out.

"Not so fast," a voice snarled and Guardians either side of them clamped heavy handcuffs on their wrists.

The Chief Guardian, dressed entirely in black and wearing a white mask with a smiling face approached. "You've invaded my domain," the synthesized voice said, "but I knew if I waited long enough you would step into my trap."

"Who are you?" Crystal demanded. "Who dares to restrain us and enslave the country folk?"

"Come now," the voice crackled. "My dear Crystal surely you should know? Crystal Charin, Business Person of the Year, you only have one enemy."

"I don't understand," Crystal protested.

"Perhaps you will when I enslave your beloved husband."

"Just try it," Sac warned.

The Chief Guardian turned towards him. "My dear boy, you have been a sharp thorn in my side since you first came to the Valley, with your compact sounds centres and marketing skills, but who are you? Nothing but an upstart who crawled out of the devastated back streets of London after the war. You are nothing more than a slum kid, you don't deserve to walk the ground of the Valley."

"You know a lot about me, who are you?" Sac demanded. "What are you so afraid of that you have to hide behind a mask and a voice synthesizer?"

"I don't have to hide. Look, if you dare at the face of your enemy." The Chief Guardian cast off the heavy black cloak and pulled the white smiley mask off.

"Penny!" Crystal and Sac cried in unison.

"And didn't it take a long time for your small brains to work out that I, and only I, could have conjured up such a brilliant plan? You walked straight into my hands. I've been monitoring you from the moment you invaded my mountain hide-out."

She turned around and beckoned one of her computer programmers to her side. "See I reward those who serve me well, don't I Rumble Byteskin?" And she tapped him affectionately on the shoulder.

"Yes, madam," he replied dutifully.

"Go with the Guardians to recover the workers, I need them for the mine and take extra supplies of obedience gas, you may need it. And deal with those four CSI associates at the bottom of the elevator shaft on your way.

"At once madam," and he scooted off to do her bidding.

Penny stretched out her hands, clenched her long shocking pink nails claw-like and drew closer to Crystal. "Why are you so pretty?"

Crystal didn't reply but took a step backwards trying to put more space between herself and her step-mother.

"I am beautiful," Penny boasted, "everyone says so."

"Everyone?" Sac asked, "how can you say everyone?"

"The Valley is now in my power," Penny chuckled. "Those greedy fools actually believe they can be young again."

"You're as bad as them," Crystal said, "because you crave eternal youth and beauty too."

"Ha," Penny smirked. "Think you can catch me in my own trap, do you? I may not be as young as you, but I alone have true beauty."

"Rubbish," Crystal shouted, "I think you're ugly."

Penny threw her head back and let loose a dreadful howl.

"You're ugly Penny, ugly," Sac chanted and Crystal joined him as they continued to call, "Ugly, ugly, ugly."

"Silence," Penny cried, "I can prove I am the most beautiful of them all." And she turned to the computer terminal and keyed in her secret password. The monitor sprang to life. "Spiegel, Spiegel, who is the most beautiful of them all?"

Crystal stared at Sac in silence. Penny had contacted Spiegel thus giving him access to the Health Farm for the first time. Crystal swallowed deeply, closed her eyes and concentrated her thoughts. Somehow she had to try to communicate with Spiegel using thought waves.

"Spiegel," Penny cried, "Who is the most beautiful of them all? Answer me!"

"Why my mistress is the most beautiful of them all," he said and Penny smiled triumphantly.

"You wanted proof," she said, her mouth twisting into a self-satisfied smile. "Now you've heard it. Spiegel is the most powerful computer known in the Valley. He always tells the truth."

"Madam," Spiegel said, "forgive the interruption but there is a problem in the production plant requiring your immediate attention."

"What," she glared at the monitor, "what do you know of this?"

"I have just intercepted a signal from a small computer unit," he replied.

"Put it on screen," she ordered. Live pictures of the Body Cream production plant appeared on the monitor. Something had gone wrong with the packaging unit and surplus Body Cream was spilling over the machinery.

"Send a Guardian," she cried.

"They are pursuing the workers," Spiegel said, "as ordered."

"Never here when wanted, I suppose I'll have to attend to this myself." And she left.

As soon as Penny was out of earshot, Spiegel answered Crystal telepathic signal. "Message received and understood," he said and the pincer grips flew open releasing both Crystal and Sac.

"Can you access the Health Farm network?" Crystal asked Spiegel.

"Negative, I only have a communication circuit open, a human hacker is required at Penny's work station."

Crystal looked quickly at Sac. "I'll stay, you go."

"No," he protested, "I'll not leave you."

"Only Crystal has the skill to re-program the production plant to self-destruct. You must go Sac and lead the workers out of the mountain."

"But I can't leave."

"You must," Crystal said. "Try to find Sam and Seth, and warn the others. I'll release the force field boundary surrounding this place as soon as I have located the correct programming, then we can all escape."

"No, it is too dangerous for you to remain—"

"I must, I need to hack into Penny's base computer. With Spiegel's help I know I can do it. It's our only chance to squash Penny and her Mesmerize empire for good."

Sac threw his arms around her and kissed her passionately. "Take care, my love, take care," he said as he released her and went in search of the others.

Crystal worked at a furious pace. First she accessed the security network and re-programmed the boundary defence co-ordinates. Then she turned her attention to the production plant which proved far more difficult to break into, but with Spiegel's help she managed to set all the production units to self-destruct.

"What is Penny's current location?" she asked Spiegel.

"Leaving packing unit and stepping inside main elevator."

"Are we nearly finished?" she asked.

"Affirmative."

"How did you get there?" Penny shouted as she breezed into the room. "And where is that worthless husband of yours?"

"Escaped." Crystal smiled. "And you are finished Penny, this time for good."

"You little fool, it will take more than you to defeat the great Penny Hacker."

"But you are beaten Penny because what you do is evil. You seek power for your own ends, not to achieve anything good or worthwhile for humanity. You had beauty and great talent once, but you wasted it because you became corrupt inside until everyone turned against you, even my father."

"That whelp!" Penny scoffed. "He was like a puppy scurrying around my feet. No man lives who is a match for me."

"Dense loved you. Did his love mean nothing to you?"

"He was weak. I loathe weakness."

Crystal thought for a few moments, she needed to keep Penny away from the computer work station for as long as possible. The longer she could keep Penny talking, the more time the others had to escape. Soon Penny would realise the security force field was down and production of Body Cream was sabotaged. She had to prevent her finding out for as long as possible.

"I am intrigued," Crystal said, "how did you escape from prison?"

"Those stupid wardens let me go," she laughed.

"But how?"

"Like the rest of the pampered residents of the Valley, they wanted my greatest invention, Body Cream."

"But it doesn't work," Crystal acted bemused. "It contains obedience gas, which you might have discovered but you didn't invent, did you? You get it from this mountain. But you are so arrogant you think that you can take over people's minds by appealing to their vanity. You're the vain one, Penny, you!"

"I don't have to listen to this. I should have killed you when I had the chance, instead out of the kindness of my heart I had you banned from the Valley."

"Then what are you waiting for?" Crystal leapt from the computer station and ran to the middle of the command room. "Come and get me, if you dare."

But Crystal wasn't fast enough Penny caught up with her and dug her sharp hot pink talons into Crystal's throat.

Crystal felt the finger nails digging into her soft skin. Her step-mother was trying to strangle her. She coughed and gasped as Penny squeezed tighter. Then summoning up all her strength, she brought her arms up and flung Penny to the ground. "Now Spiegel," Crystal cried fighting for breath and hoping she had reprogrammed the force field co-ordinates correctly.

"Spiegel obeys me..."

Penny's last words echoed around the command room as she was frozen in time, trapped by the force field she had generated to protect her Mesmerize empire.

Crystal sank to the floor, coughing and gasping for air. She managed to utter two words, "Thanks Spiegel," before a great shroud of darkness engulfed her.

Chapter Ten

Spiegel's Party

When Crystal woke up she was being cradled in Sac's arms.

"For one moment I thought I'd lost you," he breathed a deep sigh of relief.

"You...came back," she croaked.

"The others have escaped and they're heading down the mountain."

"The Guardians...Rumble-"

"Overpowered by obedience gas," Sac smiled. "And if you don't come with me now, I'll spray you with it."

Crystal offered no resistance as Sac lifted her to her feet. "Spiegel," she whispered, "activate the self-destruct program."

"Affirmative mistress," he replied.

Perhaps there should have been a huge reception in the Valley for the heroes when they returned from the mountain Health Farm. But there wasn't as hardly anyone in the Valley was aware of what had happened. The *Daily Byte* did carry a headline, "Penny Hacker escapes goal."

Crystal and Sac were going to give the Governor a full report of their mission. But once they were home, they decided the Valley was better off without Penny and so they vowed to tell no one where she was.

Rumble Byteskin and his assistant Guardians were brought to trial, sentenced and detained at the computer fraud detention centre. The true story of the Great Child Disaster did come out when Mrs Byteskin hoping to get clemency for her husband confessed her part in looking after the Valley children in the mountain. At least Governor Pip's name was cleared of the crime and a statue of him commissioned to stand in front of Government House.

Penny Hacker was blamed for almost everything, but not until Crystal and the Seven had succeeded in destroying every last container of Body Cream in the Valley.

By activating the self-destruct program at the Health Farm manufacturing plant, Spiegel had ensured no more Body Cream could be produced. However, no more Body

Cream wasn't very popular in the Valley, so the new Governor decided to have a substitute manufactured without the obedience gas ingredient.

People clamoured to buy it again and they spent a great deal of time admiring themselves. But eventually, most of them got fed up, realised the product didn't work and someone had been making fools out of them. No one likes to be made to look foolish, do they? So the Valley residents went back to work.

The country folk from the mountains soon recovered from obedience gas. They were a sturdy lot. All they needed was fresh air in their lungs again. But their old homes had been destroyed when Penny built her mountain Health Farm. So, Dense let them all move into the Hacker-White mansion, of course it was Spiegel's home too, but he didn't mind their company as the mansion did have a new twenty room extension.

At last everything returned to normality in the Valley, even the weather. So Spiegel decided to have a party. It might seem strange to anyone outside the Valley that a computer should have a party, but not to the Valley residents.

"It is my birthday," Spiegel said, "on the many invitations he sent out via the Valley social network.

The problem most people then faced was what can you give a computer for its birthday?

The Seven got their heads together and gave him seven problems to solve, but he finished them in seconds. Dense played Galactic Battleships with him for five minutes, but Dense got fed up as Spiegel always won. Sac gave him a new sound synthesizer, which he really wanted. And the country folk cleaned and polished him until he shone. Finally there was one present left. It was from Crystal.

"Aren't you going to look inside my present?" she asked him.

"I am thinking," he replied.

"Thinking," she said in a surprised tone, "surely the most advanced computer of his type in the Valley doesn't need to think for long?"

"You flatter me Crystal. I am older than you think."

"Really, now look inside my present and tell me how old you are."

Spiegel attached his sensors to the box. "323 years 5 months 8 days and 10 minutes," he said.

"So how do you like your present?"

"The circuitry is excellent, but I have no need of a lie detector. I never lie."

"That's not true," she protested, "I remember you lied to Penny."

"Negative, I am programmed to tell the truth."

"But, you told her she was the most beautiful of them all."

"I did not mean her."

"But you said your mistress was--"

"She is," he cut in, "Crystal have some more Champagne."

Now at the end of this long tale what happened to Penny Hacker? She's still where Spiegel and Crystal left her frozen in time inside her own force field. And it's quite likely that's where she'll stay to live happily ever after.

TWENTY-FOUR BLACKBIRDS

"It's a bit dark in here," Nigel moaned.

"Shhh.., you're not supposed to make a sound until the lid comes off."

"But we've been in here for ages."

"Yes, and thank the good bird lord that we're at the top and not one of those poor sods down there, dead, plucked and stewed."

"But I don't understand Alfie, what are we supposed to do?"

"Look lad, I've already told you once, as soon as the pie lid comes off, we have to fly out and chirp like there's no tomorrow and everybody will cheer and say how wonderful the king's birthday celebration is, then with a bit of luck, we make a dash for an open window before the bird-catcher can get his net around you again."

"Right, I think I can remember...er...could you just go through the bit about the window? Erm...I mean, what's a window?"

"Good grief, didn't your parents teach you anything?"

"Well I think they did...they must have but I can't quite remember."

"Trust me, twenty-four of us in this pie and I have to get stuck next to the bird with half a brain. Just follow me lad, when I say go. He who flies highest and fastest is likely to get out of this castle."

"Ok, I'll wait for your signal."

"And one more tip, when the big blade comes in do remember to duck, otherwise, it'll have your head off and then you won't be flying anywhere."

"Right, duck and then screech and then fly. You're very clever Alfie, have you done this before?"

"Course I have lad, this is my fifth time."

"And you've got away every time?"

"Wouldn't be here now if I hadn't, would I? Each time I've managed to fly out of the pie, but I've never got outside the castle, never found it yet."

"Found what, Alfie?"

"An open window duff head. Now listen, if you do find yourself up top and can't get out, let the bird-catcher get you or he'll call in the cross-bow men and they'll shoot you.

Happened to a good friend of mine on my third run, poor bugger dropped like lead and the dogs got him. Not that he knew much about it."

"You're very brave Alfie, escaping so many times. What's your secret?"

"Step on a rookie like you, of course, now go!"

HOUSE HUNTING

A well-maintained end town house, approximately five years old with a short drive, space for one vehicle, neatly trimmed lawn, flower borders, pleasant outlook – positive kerb appeal. Exactly the property I had been looking for. I paused for a brief window observation – no one inside. When I spotted the security camera I froze, until I realised it was non-functional. So, I squeezed by the side hedge and checked around the back.

The imaginative use of a small space impressed me. A stylish table and chairs stood on freshly painted decking. The garden looked easy to maintain with gravel beds and shrubs. I noted the added bonus - no sign of dogs. But when I spied the cat flap in the kitchen door I felt a wide grin spread across my face. Hmm...I pressed against it hopefully, but it didn't move. Tougher action required. I took a few steps back and shoulder charged the entrance. Useless. Seeing no point in doing myself an injury, I retraced my steps to the front door. Squatted on my haunches and waited for the owner.

Soon, a white van with lettering on the side pulled onto the drive. I stood up and raised my tail to give my prospective new owner my very best feline welcome. Bending to my level, she reached out to me. "Where have you come from?"

I lifted my head. Her touch was so soft especially around the sensitive sides of my jaw. Purr...she had made a good start.

"Fancy a saucer of milk?"

As if she needed to ask! I'd been outside for three days and nights. The scraps of pizza I'd shared with the Fire Station cat tasted vile, but I was too hungry to turn them down. When new owner unlocked the door, I slipped inside and made for the kitchen, where I waited expectantly. A few sniffs of the air convinced me this property would be ideal for me. No pet residents, despite the cat flap, not yet.

A saucer of the white stuff appeared. It wasn't full cream, so I guessed she was the healthy-living type. The only bad milk I know is no milk, although I do know some cats who get bellyache from the lactose but not me. So I lapped up the skimmed, whilst she took off her padded jacket and thick leather work boots.

"Shower," she said. I watched her scamper upstairs through the open treads as a cold shiver ran down my backbone. I shuddered. I don't do water.

I thought about making a dash for the front door but she'd closed it behind her. I waited at the foot of the stairs, then saw her flash by in the nude. She closed the bathroom door and I breathed a sigh of relief. The shower was for her. Time to have another look around, so I sneaked into the lounge-diner. Minimalist, or that chap Feng Shui had done her decorating – plain walls, laminate floors and two matching leather sofas and several large cardboard boxes. Had she just moved in or was she moving on? That worried me.

I sauntered into the hall looking for any further rooms but I'd covered them all on the ground floor. My reflection in the hall mirror gave me a start. How had I let myself get so scruffy? Time to go to basic grooming mode.

I guess she had finished her shower as she bounced down the stairs looking white and fluffy in a towelling dressing gown and smelling of flowers. Trying to be friendly I leg brushed her. She liked that. Women are so easy to please. I can't understand why men are always moaning about how difficult it is to impress them. My prospective new owner was shaping up nicely, but would she let me stay?

"I moved in last week," she said, "where do you belong?" Her voice almost purred as she gave my coat a sensual stroke and rubbed her thumb across the bridge of my nose. Wow! Had I really hit pay dirt this time?

"Meow," I replied, that's cat talk for "me stay." But she must have thought I wanted to feed. She went straight to the fridge and gave me some chicken. When I'd devoured every delicious morsel, I found a warm place where her central heating pipes ran under the flooring and snuggled down for the night. I guessed she wasn't the sort of woman who would want me in her bedroom, not on my first night.

Next I heard the hall clock strike. She switched off the TV, scooped me up and lobbed me out of the back door. I landed on the decking and shook myself. Obviously she wanted me to attend to my domestics, so I made use of her back garden. Then I took up position near her back door and waited to be invited inside.

It didn't take me long to realise I was out in the cold again for another night. Worse, it started to rain. I had a choice, hang around or try to find another billet. But as I'm the persistent type I decided to stick around and keep to my original plan. The house was so perfect for me, I couldn't let it go. If I hung around for a few days, perhaps she would grasp the fact that I needed a new home too, and take me in. It was worth a gamble.

I sheltered under her decking for a few hours, but a familiar smell kept making my nose and whiskers twitch. The rain clouds parted and shafts of moonlight flooded through the gaps in the decking. A slight movement in the corner caught my eye. I wasn't alone. Four mice were crouched around a flat pebble. As I crept closer they started an argument and failed to notice my presence. The fattest was doing most of the talking. His dominant squeak got louder. He claimed the rights to the decking area with his wife. He told the younger couple to move on. I edged nearer but couldn't see his whiskery face. His skinny tail quivered as he poised to throw the youngsters off his patch.

I, too, was poised but for a different reason. My tongue began to salivate in anticipation of a warm, late night supper. Four at once was too challenging and downright greedy. Fat Mouse and his wife were my targets. I needed to be bold. Surprise was my advantage, but I had to strike fast and go for the kill, instead of playing my usual teasing game.

"This is my house," he squeaked, "there's

no room here for the likes of you, even if she is pregnant."

That was my signal to pounce. I floored Fat Mouse with one swipe of my paw and held him on the ground. Mrs Fat Mouse died instantly as I sank my teeth into her throat. The younger couple ran for their lives. I swallowed Mrs Fat Mouse whole as her husband dithered beneath my right paw. Around dawn he breathed his last.

I resumed my position at new owner's back door with my trophy pinned beneath my outstretched paw. It was a big gamble. What if she loved all animals and chastised me for slaughtering her decking mates? On the other hand, she might welcome me with open arms as her vermin slaying champion. I gave the cat flap a push, no luck, it was still bolted. Then I heard movement inside the house, so I let out a cry, nothing too alarming, just enough to draw her attention.

She opened the door and looked down at me and my trophy. "Have you been there all night? Been doing a bit of hunting, have we?"

I replied by pushing the dead mouse towards her. In true I-wannabe-your-champion style, I offered her my prize kill. It was crunch-time. My future home lay in the balance. I wanted the house and I liked her, but if we were to be compatible house-mates she would have to accept some of my ways. I gave the dead mouse another gentle push towards her, I wanted to make it perfectly clear I'm a hunter not a gatherer.

"For me?"

"Meow."

"I'll bag it up."

I wasn't sure what she meant, but as she had left the door open, I went inside. I sat down where she had given me the milk and chicken pieces the previous night. Perhaps she'd get the hint and find me some breakfast in exchange for the nice fat mouse I'd given her. She followed me inside, slipped on a pair of thick rubber gloves and went outside again. I watched her lift the corpse into a small black pouch, double wrap it and place it in the dustbin. What a waste! Didn't she know she was throwing away good rodent meat? She gave me a saucer of milk – skimmed, I suppose I'll get used to it.

"Who do you belong to?" But without waiting for an answer she grabbed my tail and lifted my hind legs in the air. Can't say I liked her doing that, but when she muttered: "Oh, I see you've been done!" I realised she referred to my masculine loss. If only she'd asked I would have told her my first owner had taken care of that when I was younger. But my prospective owner didn't seem to have much of a handle on cat speak. I'd have to teach her.

As I had her attention, I paraded around

her kitchen, keeping to the floor area. I understood kitchen ground rules, gleaming granite-surfaced worktops and muddy paws do not create harmony. Her kitchen had the wow-factor, high gloss white units and a sparkling cooking range. I knew these were no-go areas, so I stopped suddenly and feigned surprise at my own reflection.

"Silly puss," she said and picked me up. "I'll get you to the vets. Find out if you're micro-chipped. I'll ask the neighbours. See if they know anything about you." She stroked my head with her index finger. "Want to stay Partner?"

"Meow," I replied. The stay part sounded good, the house already felt like home. I'd even agree to wear a collar if she provided me with my own bed and fixed the cat flap. But I wasn't sure about the Partner bit, was that to be my new name?

Her mobile rang. "Essential Pest Control Services," she replied.

"Cat," said the voice, "it's Andy from Acme Estate Agency. Can you do an emergency call-out for us today?"

MUM'S THE WORD

Let me introduce myself, I'm Danvers, I do have a first name but no one ever uses it. Just plain Danvers will do. I've worked at the palace for five years. I first came on work experience. This teacher at school said there was a place for a footman or 'footboy' as he called them and thought I'd be the right lad for the job. Being wet behind the ears I had no notion or what a "footboy" actually did but I soon found out.

I was assigned to the prince's apartment, which looking back was the best thing that could have happened. My work was fairly straightforward and two weeks of work experience flashed by. On the last day I was real sad to go back to school and the prince must have noticed how unhappy I looked. He asked me how old I was.

"Sixteen sir," I replied.

"When you're eighteen come back and work for me."

I was gobsmacked and Mum was delighted when I got home and told her I had a job offer at the palace. I didn't do much after leaving school until I was eighteen, but then I didn't need to, did I?

Okay, so what sort of work do I do now? I serve food, I polish candlesticks, I download all the stuff from the internet that I'm told to and I make sure the prince is up-to-date with his social media.

There are days when he doesn't say anything, that's when I have to work hard creating interesting stuff for him. Of course, none of it goes out under his real name that would be stupid, wouldn't it? Okay, so life was real cool until the king decided it was time for the prince to marry. All about maintaining their line and producing an heir and so on.

The prince didn't like that idea at bit. Well he wouldn't would he? I mean he and the head footman and the rest of us footboys, we're one big happy family, aren't we?

The prince stormed into his apartment. "What am I going to do?" he cried. "My parents are organising a super ball, inviting all the eligible girls in the country, insisting that I choose one of them and marry her. It doesn't matter which one I choose, as long as I pick one of them to be my wife."

The head footman turned puce. "Oh my God, does that mean we've all got to clear out?"

"Over my dead body," the prince replied.

"But sir, what are you going to do?" the head footman asked.

They paced the room, each coming up with the most stupid ideas imaginable.

"Excuse me, sir," I said, "but did you say all the eligible girls in the country would be invited?"

"Yes, so what?"

"Can't I dress as a girl? If I came to the ball, you could fall in love with me, and we could be married and live happily ever after, all of us sir, just like now."

"How can you convince my parents you're a girl?"

"Well, I saw a fairy advert on the net a few days ago. It said, instant make-over, realise your potential, gain confidence, nothing's impossible. Look good, whoever you are."

"Splendid! Get onto it," the prince commanded.

That's how I got to the ball. The invitation was easy. As for the make-over, it was painful but I was on my way to the ball, pink coach, four white horses – the full works. My dress was gossamer fine and fluffy. Some might say a bit on the meringue side but I had to make an impression, didn't I?

I glided into the ballroom and floated down the grand staircase and yes, the prince was there. He picked me out and refused to dance with anyone else in the room. It was arranged for me to run off at the stroke of twelve. We had to do that, the prince had promised his footboys a private party in his apartment later that night. Well, it was the least he could do, they'd been there for hours taking an interest in the hoards of eligible young girls the King and Queen had invited. The head footman, give him his due, had danced his socks off.

Once I got clear of the palace gates, I slung my crystal shoe out of the window. We hid the coach and four in the woods and legged it back to the prince's apartment. Wow! What a grand party that was. We let it be known that the prince was bereft that the lovely princess had done a runner and we partied until dawn.

Next day, the palace was overrun with proclamations - go here, do that, the prince will search the land for the princess he has fallen in love with and so on. The media buzzed, the internet sizzled and our mobiles inside the prince's apartment didn't stop ringing.

A few days later we staged the discovery. I wore a more subdued ragged number. We thought the poverty angle was a brilliant idea. I was found slaving away in a kitchen where I'd been suppressed by my two older sisters.

They were played by two of our footboys who used to be actors.

Well, we had a beautiful wedding which was celebrated throughout the land. Some of the press reports did hint that I wasn't perhaps the most beautiful bride to grace the royal household, but that was a far as they dared go.

And did we live happily ever after? Yes, of course, nothing had changed in the prince's big happy family. However, a few months on there's a lot of hinting about the royal line. So, that's my current project. I'm searching the internet for a surrogate and I've named it Mum's-the-Word. Don't know of any suitable candidates for the job, do you?

THE TOY BOY'S TALE

Thanks for the drink. The name's Adam and officially I'm a gardener but...and you will keep this quiet won't you? I'm a toy boy.

I work for Mrs Cougar–White up at the Manor. She's a very demanding woman in more ways than one, I can tell you. But we're living in tough economic times these days, and a man's got to find work where he can, if he's to survive.

You're probably thinking I've got an easy job. No way! Madam's got a sore temper on her I can tell you when she let's rip. No mate, I'd challenge the strongest bloke to stand up to her when she's got her blood riled. She's married but nobody sees much of him. He's known hereabouts as *him-in-doors*. Folks say he's feeble-minded or lost what little brain he once had. It's also rumoured he's dead. But there ain't been a funeral and none of the other staff have ever mentioned seeing a dead body hanging around the place. My guess is he's still about somewhere, but I haven't seen him at the Manor all the time I've been working for her.

'Course, there's been other rumours about her, guessed you might have heard a few, you being here and all, asking questions. Why only last week when I was having a pint here in The Tales, just like now, this bloke says, 'Is Mrs Cougar-White a witch and does she have an all-seeing mirror?'

'You been eating those magic mushrooms from the forest floor, haven't you?' I nudged him.

'Dunno what you're talking about,' says he, 'but I've heard as Mrs Cougar-White can see into the future and that's how she makes her money.'

'Perhaps she can,' says I, shrugging my shoulders and not wanting to let on too much, 'but she's never told me about my future. I mean a few racing tips, or winning lottery numbers wouldn't go amiss.'

Anyway, he didn't seem to get the joke as he ups and leaves without buying me a drink. That was his loss, I remember thinking at the time, because I'd have told him a tale if he'd stood me a pint, like you.

Now, everything was pretty normal

around here until one day last year when Mrs Cougar-White says to me, 'Adam, what do you know about the whereabouts of the brothers Green?'

'The ugly bunch, who live together up at Seven Hills,' I said. She nodded. 'They call themselves eco-warriors and they re-cycle everything and I do mean everything. Just imagine it, all of them in the same house. They've got no running water, and that cottage is only a one up, one down – rooms, that is.'

'How they live is their business,' she said, 'but I've heard they're not alone, what do you know?'

Now I thought that was a bit odd, I mean, she's supposed to be the one with the all-seeing mirror and she's asking me! Surely, everybody knows I'm only employed because of my...good looks. I scratched my head, trying to work out what she really wanted to know. I've learnt to tell her what she wants to hear. It never fails. 'They live off the land and grow all their own stuff. Some say they've got a pretty housekeeper, but I reckon that's just talk.'

The word 'pretty' seemed to make her cringe. Her eyes narrowed and turned black. I could see she was cooking something up. 'Bring me the finest apple you've grown,' she said. Now, I thought that was odd as she don't eat fruit. But whatever Mrs Cougar-White wants, she gets, so I went and picked one from the orchard. When I gave it to her she said, 'Guard my door with your life. Let no one pass, not even my husband!'

Now that was a turn up because I wouldn't have recognised him if I'd seen him. But on guard I stood. Hours later, I was still there, leaning against her door long after my shift should have finished. But I daren't leave, just in case she...needed me. Well, you understand, it's what I'm paid for.

I must have nodded off because suddenly I was woken up by a horrendous commotion inside her room. Talk about waking the dead, it sounded like all hell had been let loose. As if hundreds of voices were moaning, groaning and wailing. But the most frightening part was hearing her shouting above them in the foulest language I'd ever heard. Part of me wanted to run away, another bit of me was tempted to go inside. I didn't know what to do, or what I might find if I pushed the door ajar. I didn't want to get on her wrong side, but curiosity got the better of me. I crouched down and peered through the keyhole.

Horrible goblins were running around the room, jumping about and screeching. A giant cockroach had his antennae stirring a giant pot of bubbling goo in the middle of the room. Mrs Cougar-White, dressed all in black with a green mask covering her lovely face, was reeling off what sounded like an incantation of some sort. Then she stands over the cauldron of goo and slings in the nice rosy apple I'd brought her. Zapp! A shout and they were gone. The room was empty except for her, standing there in one of her nice evening gowns, the black garb, now, pooled around her feet.

Backing away from her door, I sat down on the floor and waited. Eventually I heard the door creak open and her long slender hand beckoned me inside.

Being an obliging sort of bloke, I went in. The goblins and the giant cockroach were out of there, of course. Thankfully, it was just her and me. All through the night she asked me again and again, 'Who's the most beautiful woman in the world?'

'Course I told her it was her, that's what she wanted to hear. She pays me well and there's added perks, but I can't go into details, you understand?

After that, things went pretty quiet for a few months until another odd rumour started about a shrine up at Seven Hills. People said there was a big see-through coffin up there containing a beautiful young woman, guarded twenty-four seven by the Green brothers. Everyone thought the woman was dead, her being in her coffin, but strangely, her body hadn't decayed. I was going to tell Mrs Cougar-White, but when I learnt the coffin bore an inscription, 'Here lies Blaise White,' I thought again. She was *him-in-doors'* only child, by his first wife. But that girl had died years ago in the forest. By all accounts there'd been a big funeral. Very sad it was, they said, her being so young. Some say that's what upset *him-in-doors,* the loss of his daughter made him senile, but I don't know about that having never clapped eyes on him. I thought it best not to say anything to Mrs Cougar-White, as I didn't want to send her into one of her rages. Instead, I decided to investigate myself.

Phew! It wasn't half a long way up that valley, I thought I'd never get to Seven Hills. I was having a rest when I saw a good-looking young bloke with the Green brothers coming down the hill carrying the said coffin. Sure enough inside was a body, but she didn't look dead, just asleep. Now that was mighty strange, wasn't it?

The track was steep and full of potholes so I wasn't surprised when the littlest of the brothers trips over. The next one followed him and before you knew it, they'd all piled on top of one another. 'Course the eco-friendly coffin made out of recycled goodness-knows-what slid out of their grasp, hit the ground and bio-degraded into thousands of pieces.

And if I'd not seen it myself, I'd never have believed it - the young woman came back to life!

The good-looking bloke went down on his knees. 'Beloved Blaise,' he said, 'I fell in love with you when I saw you in the eco-friendly, bio-degradable, recycled coffin.'

Who was this weirdo? Who goes around falling in love with dead bodies?

'Let me take you away from this place,' he went on.

She must have been a bit dazed, which is quite understandable being shut away in a recycled box for months without any food or water. Mind you, she didn't look too bad on it, in fact, she was something of a stunner. But I think the brothers should have stepped in. Did she know him? And where was he offering to take her?

'Come home with me,' I heard him say, 'marry me.'

Now *that* convinced me he was a complete nutter. Who in their right mind proposes to a woman he's just met? Especially one that's come back from the dead!

And what were the eco-warriors doing whilst all this lovey-dovey action was going on? I'll tell you, trying to get the little 'un out of a deep hole, that's what. They were pulling, pushing and shoving him, and still he was stuck. I felt obliged to help. Being a tall, strapping lad myself, I had no difficulty getting him out.

'Praise be, I'm eternally grateful to you sir,' he panted, shaking soil from his clothes.

'I'm no sir,' I told him, 'just plain Adam will do.'

'Whatever you calls your good self, I and my six brothers will remain grateful to you until you draw your last breath.'

'I hope that's not too soon,' I said.

Of course, all this went by our new-found lovers, who were locked in each other's arms like they'd been matched for compatibility on the internet.

'My head aches,' she moaned, 'and I'm so thirsty.'

He whips out a hip flask and offers it to her. Whether it contained water or something stronger, I couldn't say as he didn't offer anybody else a swig.

'Come back to our cottage,' the oldest brother said.

I didn't fancy being surrounded by all their recycled rubbish, so I shook my head, 'I've got a long journey back home,' I told him, 'but you will look after her, won't you? Only it seems a bit odd she's going off with some bloke she's only just met.'

The eldest Green brother scratched his beard, 'We don't want her to leave. We've looked after her since she fled from her step-mother, the witch with the all-seeing mirror. If the witch knows she's alive, she might come after her again. The witch tried to kill our Blaise and we thought she'd succeeded when we found the poisoned apple.'

It didn't take me long to realise Mrs Cougar-White had been up to a few tricks. And I did feel a bit guilty about the apple, not that I had anything to do with poison, you understand? 'What are you going to do?' I asked them.

'Don't know,' they shook their heads. 'We tried to protect her,' said the eldest, 'but we can't shield her from black magic.'

'Come home with me to Silicon Valley,' the young man declared. 'In the land of computer circuits black magic has been debugged. You'll be safe there Blaise, and you Green brothers and you good sir.'

'Adam,' I replied, 'thank you for the offer. But I have responsibilities here and I don't think I'd fit in.'

So off they went. The brothers singing some eco chant, and Blaise all smiles for her new bloke.

And me?

I'm still here to tell the tale at the pub to anyone who cares to listen except Mrs Cougar-White. I'm not stupid. Anyway, she can find out for herself, can't she? After all, ain't she got an all-seeing mirror?

ISME AND ME

She appeared, as she always does as soon as the Sun goes down on October 31st – Halloween.

She looked older, as she always does, and uglier than last year. But with her black ragged clothes and that pointy hat, no one will take a scrap of notice out on the street tonight, until they see her face.

I've tried to get away from her. I moved to London and I was very happy there, except every Halloween. As usual, she insisted on following me around, on the tube, in the bar, at a drinks party and she scares people, especially blokes. Of course, that makes me furious. I can't shake her off and I know I should have been resigned to her after all these years, but I'm not.

"Isme, you look ghastly!"

"Ooo, thank you dear, I thought you'd never notice. It's my skin, you know." She touches her parchment-like, green face pocked with warts with her elongated, bony finger. Sheets of dead skin shower onto the floor.

"Don't do that! I'll have to deal with your mess tomorrow when you've gone."

"Haven't you got a cleaner?" Isme spits out two teeth onto the mole hill of skin she's already shed. "Now, where are we going tonight?"

"Nowhere, we're staying in."

She howls like a pack of werewolves on heat, an obliging fork of lightning flashes outside and an ear-blasting clap of thunder follows. "Isme, there's no need to get angry."

"Angry? I don't do angry. That's you, I've no need to get angry, have I?"

I eyeball her and try to stare her out. But she wins and I shift my gaze away.

"Please, let's go out," she says, "we always do. And this is the most wonderful night of the year. I'm so desperate to get a bit of action."

"No,"

"But, I've got no other time...and I've been looking forward to it so much."

"I know you have," I twitch my nose and buff my nails.

"It's not fair. You have the rest of the year, to do whatever you like and I...I've only got tonight."

"Well," I shrug, "That's not my problem."

"Ugh! Why do you have to be so mean?"

I laugh until the tears roll down my cheeks and my sides ache. Eventually, I give in. "Alright, let's get on your broomstick and pay a visit to that fat guy up in Lapland."

Isme jumps to her feet, brings her broomstick to heel and invites me to hop on. "Oh!" she cries as we zoom northwards towards Santa Clauses' hideout. "What made you think of him?"

"Yesterday, I saw our Halloween stuff being shoved to the back of a store and his jingle, red nosed, glittery garbage given prime location. Besides, we've not seen him for a hundred years."

"Do you think he'll recognise us?" She asks as we cross the coast of Finland.

"Of course he'll recognise me, I haven't changed a bit. As for you? Not a chance."

"Ooo! Do I really look so horrible?"

"Isme, you are now so bad, anyone who looks at your face will most likely go mad on the spot."

"Really, am I that vile?"

"Yes dear, I've worked very hard over the years to get you looking so gross."

We land badly on the ice. Isme breaks her arm and it hangs by a thread like a dead branch on a tree. "I'll go in first," I push her out of the way as we approach his log cabin. "You wait here, when I give you the signal, burst in and give him one of your spine-chilling stares."

Isme nods, "What's the signal?"

"Halloween, of course, as always."

I trudge through the snow to Santa's door. I expected one of his helpers might have been out and cleared a pathway, but no, not an elf or reindeer in sight. I wish I'd given this trip a bit more thought, as my gold Jimmy Choos are ruined.

As there's nobody about I don't bother to knock. Besides, he's not the sort to lock his door, after all how many personal callers does he get these days, anyway?

I breeze in. "Hello Santa." But what a shock? I thought Isme looked haggard earlier, but this old man was way past his sell-by-date. It took him all his time to look up at me.

"Who's there?" he asks.

"Don't you recognise me?" I step closer to him and shiver. His cabin is cold. There's only a pathetic single flame burning in the hearth.

"No, am I supposed to?" he replies.

"You should, I've come miles to see you, specially."

"Have you? Wasting your time, I'm not in the business anymore."

"What? But the stores are full of your stuff, already and it's only Halloween."

Damn, I didn't mean to call the signal word so quickly, but there's no way back. Isme breaks down the door with one lightning strike, broomstick in hand she glares at Santa. Nothing happens. I glare at her. She lets out another cackle but Santa's unmoved.

"Who's that?" he asks.

"It's Isme, my alter ego," I tell him. "You're supposed to look at her diabolical face and go stark-raving mad."

"Ah," he sighs, "I remember you. You're the young woman who wanted to be a witch who never aged no matter what evil you did. 'Course I couldn't grant your wish and I guess you went elsewhere. Did you? Most likely, I suppose you can live forever now as long as you do bad things and Isme gets uglier the more wrong you--"

"Ok...so you know me. Why hasn't Isme sent you mad? I came here to prevent you doing your job, so those lovely little children will go without their Christmas presents."

"Told you. Waste of time. I've been made redundant."

"But why hasn't Isme's face worked?"

"I've gone blind and there's nothing anyone can do about it."

"But the children?"

"They'll be alright, their mums and dads will keep the magic going. The kids will get plenty of presents. The festive season is turning into a farce, these days. Come October, everybody dresses up at ghouls, witches and ghosts. I bet no one bats an eyelid when you and Isme go out tonight. And all those films about werewolves, demons, Vampires, shape-shifters, and other strange creatures, they're the norm. In a week's time, everybody's out burning guys and letting of fireworks. Then Christmas? Nobody needs me anymore. So I stay indoors and enjoy my stash of dine-in-for-two dinners. Why not join me this year instead of trying to scare the wits out of folk?"

"What about me?" Isme screeches.

"You don't eat anything." I step towards her. "Can you mend the door? There's a bit of a draft in here and do something about that fire."

Slowly, she turns around and flashes her broomstick. The door jumps back onto its hinges and smacks to with a loud thud. The fire springs to a warm blaze.

"Ah...that's better." Santa rubs his hands together. "It's nice to have company."

"This dine-in-for-two meal tastes delicious." I wash down another mouthful with a generous gulp of Beaujolais.

"It's alright for some," Isme moans.

"Shut up!" Santa and I reply in unison.

Dining over, it's time to go so I check my make-up in Santa's mirror. "Oh, horrors! I swear I'm developing a line on my face." Quickly I turn to Isme, "How do you feel?"

She stands up and re-attaches her broken limb. "Do you know, I feel years younger."

THE AUDITION

Zena put her glasses on and read the letter from the Witches' Association: *Notice is hereby given that from October 31ˢᵗ, due to rising costs, all further orders must be placed via the internet.*

"What are we going to do?" she asked Cyril, her black feline companion. "We don't do computers."

He replied with his usual disdain and yawned. Fortunately she saw a computer course for beginners advertised in the local paper and decided to sign up.

At the college she met a charming young man called Will, who took her step by step through the whole complex business of getting online.

"If you could have a wish come true," she asked him after she had successfully sent an email and logged onto a website by herself, "what would it be?"

He appeared a little taken aback by her question. "Didn't realise you were a fairy godmother," he said.

"I'm not," she replied and thought nothing could be further from the truth but she couldn't tell him. It was against the Association's rules. If she was reported, she might get struck off and that would be embarrassing. "Just curious," she said.

Will shrugged. "Money, I suppose."

"Yes, everybody wants money," Zena nodded, "but what do you really want?"

Will coloured and leaned forward to whisper in Zena's ear. "I'd like to meet a girl. A nice girl, you know, one I could get on with that liked me as much as I liked her."

"Is that all?"

"No," he coughed, "no, I mean I'd like to...oh, forget it."

But Zena didn't want to forget it and when she saw him sitting alone in the college cafe later that day, she took the seat next to him. "About this girl you'd like to meet," she said in a hushed tone. "How about that one over there?"

A pretty girl, about Will's age, sat alone in the corner. He looked at her. "She's way out of my league."

"I don't think so, why don't you go and

talk to her?"

He shook his head. "I...I wouldn't know what to say."

"Nonsense, just give it a try. You'll never know what you might have missed if you don't."

He gave her a disbelieving look. "You sound like my gran."

"Well, I'm sure she'd agree with me. Go over there and say hello. She won't bite and if she doesn't want to talk to you, what have you lost?"

Will hesitated for a few moments then got to his feet. "OK, I'll tell her Grannie Zena, my fairy god-mother sent me, shall I?"

"Good idea but just do it! Oh, dear, time's getting on. Cyril will want his supper, must dash, good luck."

Zena stood up but before she left she felt the need to powder her nose. She took her compact out of her bag and gently blew some of the contents into the air. As she left the building, she looked back through the window and saw Will and the girl, sitting close, chatting away.

The next day at the college Zena logged onto the net. This time she came armed with her access codes to the Association's website. She spent the whole morning browsing. They had many new accessories she hadn't seen before. But one especially took her eye, a brand new broom. It was the latest model, concealed as a folding walking stick, fully portable and guaranteed to cause no problem when taken through customs or when scanned by those security machines that seem to be everywhere these days.

It was rather expensive but the specification was so superior to any previous broom Zena had owned, she had to have it. She ticked the box and went to the check out page.

Delivery was promised the next day and the Association was as good as its word because at one minute past mid-night, the broom came winging its way into Zena's house. She was absolutely delighted and began practising with it immediately. Her first few flights were confined to short excursions around the garden in case of accident. Cyril was not very co-operative and refused to sit on the end of it. Instead, he wandered back to his usual seat on the old besom and watched as Zena zoomed overhead. Eventually he hopped on the new broom.

Having mastered the basic techniques, Zena explored the extra features. The broom had fingertip control. Not only could it achieve high speeds but also it was environmentally-friendly and guaranteed pollution free. Zena had bought the deluxe model which had the

Association reference book built into a small fold out screen and had certain properties previously restricted for use by senior Association members only, the complete book of spells. In all, it was the perfect accessory for a modern fashionable witch of advancing years.

A week later an article in the local newspaper caught Zena's eye: The Optico Theatre Company will be holding auditions for their new production of "The Witches" amateur actors especially welcome. Zena read it out loud to Cyril. "Do you think I'd be any good?"

Cyril replied with his usual indifference and stretched out his long body as only felines can.

"That's decided then," Zena said and popped a few things into her brand new oversized handbag, the height of fashion this season.

The next morning, she jostled for position in a long queue of ladies of somewhat mature years. They came in several shapes and sizes, and probably were all convinced they would be superb for the part. Actually, there were twelve parts. "If only I can get one," Zena thought as she waited, "preferably one with a few lines."

But she hadn't expected so many hopefuls.

The queue was so long it wrapped itself around the theatre and stretched half-way down the high street.

"This is sheer chaos," a haughty woman next to Zena said. "My agent usually arranges an appointment for me when I audition, does yours?"

"Well, I've-"

"And what did you say you've been in?" she asked but gave Zena no time to answer as she reeled off the many roles she had played.

Zena gave her a sideways look, thought she was too bossy and fished inside her bag for her new short black wand. She concealed it up her sleeve, reached out to the woman and touched her arm.

"Oh," the woman moaned, "I'm feeling rather faint. I don't think I can stand in this queue much longer. Perhaps the part's not for me." And she left.

Her departure didn't surprise Zena. "Good," she murmured under her breath, "nice to know I haven't lost my touch."

Inside the theatre Zena saw a row of ladies occupying the front seats of the stalls. Had all the parts been cast? She glanced at the remainder of the wannabe witches who were put into lines of twelve. In turn each row had to walk on stage and a voice from the auditorium called, "Turn around." They did.

"And again." They did. "Thank you, we'll let you know." And they exited via the opposite wing.

Zena decided the dull auditions needed some extra spice. She reached inside her large handbag and pulled out her brand new compact filled with special dust. As she pretended to dab a little on her nose, she blew some of it into the air, chanting under her breath.

It worked better than pollen on chronic hay fever suffers. The front row ladies developed fits of sneezing. Their noise was so loud they were ushered out by the director's assistant.

"Next," a voice in the auditorium called.

Zena looked over her shoulder. She was the only one waiting in the wings.

"Time for something really spectacular," she muttered and produced her folding walking stick. She hobbled onto the stage leaning on it, grinned at the director and raised the disguised broom.

"You're hired," he announced.

"Yes," Zena cried, punched the air with her clenched fist and danced around. Then she looked down at her new broom, ran her fingers along its length and folded it back into its compact mode. "I will enjoy playing myself on stage," she muttered, "wait 'til I tell Cyril the new broom really does sweep clean."

ABOUT THE AUTHOR

Lynda Dunwell is an LSE graduate who taught economics and business studies for over twenty years. She has also worked as a press officer, advertisement copy writer and tourist officer.

She is an award winning short story writer and historical romantic novelist. For many years the old fairy tales have fascinated her, so much she decided to gather together some of the short stories she had written into this one volume.

Although based in the landlocked English Midlands, Lynda loves the sea and spends most of her vacations on cruise ships.

She is a member of the UK Romantic Novelists' Association, the Historical Novel Society and the Jane Austen Society.

Another interest is family history. Lynda is a member of the Society of Genealogists and has traced her paternal family line – the Dunwells – back to 1485. Currently she is researching her female line which she describes as far more challenging.

Website: www.lyndadunwell.com

Or find her on facebook: LyndaDunwell and twitter @LyndaDunwell

Other Books by Lynda Dunwell

Regency Romances
Marrying the Admiral's Daughter
Captain Westwood's Inheritance
Colonel Weston's Wedding

Victorian Romance
Heart's Desire

Edwardian Romance on RMS Titanic
Tomorrow Belongs to Us

Short Story Collections

Titanic Twelve Tales